DARK WOOD
DARK WATER

DARK
WOOD
DARK WATER

TINA CALLAGHAN

POOLBEG

This novel is entirely a work of fiction. The names, characters and incidents portrayed in it are the work of the author's imagination. Any resemblance to actual persons, living or dead, events or localities is entirely coincidental.

Published 2018
by Poolbeg Press Ltd
123 Grange Hill, Baldoyle
Dublin 13, Ireland
E-mail: poolbeg@poolbeg.com

Typesetting, editing, layout, design, ebook © Poolbeg Press Ltd.

1

A catalogue record for this book is available from the British Library.

ISBN 978-1-78199-780-2

Typeset by Poolbeg

Printed and bound by CPI Group (UK) Ltd, Croydon, CR0 4YY

www.poolbeg.com

About the Author

Tina Callaghan is a writer of speculative fiction, both for children and adults. Her stories involve elements of history, mythology and the supernatural. Her short stories have appeared in anthologies alongside horror and science-fiction greats Stephen King, Dean Koontz, Ray Bradbury and Robert Bloch.

Tina lives in County Wexford with her partner Joe and lots of pets.

Dark Wood Dark Water is her debut novel.

Acknowledgements

Having love and support is important for everyone. The work (and joy) of writing a novel is made easier (and more joyful) by having people in your life who love you and believe in you, especially in those moments where you get stuck and need someone to kick you lovingly into action.

I am blessed to have wonderful people in my life. I especially want to thank my partner Joe Bradley, for just everything he does and is. I also couldn't do without my best friend Colette Somers who is the sister I never had. When we're old, she's going to have a pink rinse, and I'm going to have a blue one.

My brother Des, his wife Trish, and my wonderful niece and nephew, Hollie and Bryan, are always there for me, and now we have Robyn Rae, a new Callaghan born to Bryan and his partner Katie in 2018. Welcome, Robyn!

Thank you to my extended family and all the friends who wished me well. You guys are cool.

Imelda Carroll and Jamie Lynn Saunders, thanks for believing. You are both brilliant writers as well as good friends. Thank you, Cat Hogan, bestselling author and friend, for all your support and for screaming when I told you the news. Sarah Dixon and Maria Farrell, if I ever need people to help me with a jet-set lifestyle, you're up!

The *New Ross Standard* has been very supportive, for which I'm grateful. Special thanks go to David Looby, who has an amazing talent, both as a journalist and as a writer of superb fiction.

Thanks to Mary Browne in Browne Photography for making the experience of having an 'author picture' taken not only easy but fun.

Thank you to all the staff at Wexford Book Centre, especially Amy Devereux, young adult books supremo.

Thank you to my colleagues in Wexford Libraries for their support and their genuine delight for me when my dream came true. You all do a fantastic job and an important one.

The first person outside of my family to talk to me about being a writer was my First Year English teacher, Maeve Wilson (née Butler) in Our Lady of Lourdes Secondary School, New Ross. She told me that the most important thing was to keep the reader interested and engaged. She was right and it's the one rule I always try to stick to. Maeve passed away before I got to tell her about this book. I hope she knows now. Thank you, Miss Butler.

Although a novel is written alone, everything else involved needs a tribe and I have been incredibly lucky to find mine. Thank you for everything, Paula Campbell. You are an amazing publisher and a kindred spirit. My editor is Gaye Shortland and the woman has eagle eyes. Thanks, Gaye, for seeing the wood, despite the trees, and the trees as well.

Poolbeg is a wonderful company and I am thrilled to be joining the ranks of all the fabulous writers they have published over the years. I have been dreaming of this since I was nine. See what you've done, Poolbeg? Thank you for it.

Mam and Dad, I know you'd be as proud as punch. Thank you for stories, books and adventures. You're not here for this, but I know you're keeping an eye on us.

To Mam, for French doors and camomile lawns

Prologue

Bailey's historic old streets wind and climb and it has alleys and long sets of steps leading from the lower town to the upper. It has charm and a combination of ancient and modern that make it a pleasant and interesting place to live. And like any town, it has both bright and dark about it. And it has the river.

Bailey's river is tidal, all the way up from the sea to beyond the town and the first lock. The lock forms the barrier between the tidal river and the inland waterway. Below the lock, within reach of Bailey, the past lives.

The river is a vein of history. Its surface looks the same when viewed by modern eyes as it did to druids and warriors, to Vikings and other invading forces. The river's secrets are hidden in its mud and its elephant-slow days. It carries pleasure cruisers as it once did merchant ships. It doesn't care, or even notice. Its life is underneath and it skims the edges of its world with slow-destroying fingers. It is the lifeblood of its towns and villages but demands its forfeit. Sometimes, that is a great tree, sometimes a fallen and bloated cow, its legs sticking up out of the mud at low tide, sometimes a boat, taken in a storm. Sometimes, it demands a greater forfeit.

Sometimes, it just takes it.

Halley woke into a different age. He lay still, feeling the movement of the ship beneath him. The Zephyros *had travelled far with him as her captain. Through centuries, ghostly and barely there. He had tried so many times to change things, to stop the evil that he pursued. Nothing ever changed. And yet, now, this awakening seemed different. He felt stronger than he had done for a long time. He reached up and touched the timber of the wall behind his bed. He swung his feet over the edge and went up. The dawn was colouring the sky and the wide river drew him to Bailey as it always did. To Bailey and from it, an ebb and flow that had lasted for more years than he could count.*

There it was. The town, softly coloured in the early light, welcoming and repelling all at once. He had the strange feeling again. This time the approach felt different. There was something new about the town. Something or someone was coming with him.

Halley looked down at himself. In a flash of rising sun, he saw that his body was dressed in clothing he didn't recognise. The moment was fleeting, but he felt both himself and someone other.

He looked back up at Bailey and let the river carry him in. This time, he was smiling.

Chapter One

Callum listened at Josh's door. Not a sound from his brother. Their parents were out with friends. Callum went quietly downstairs. He couldn't sleep when he was home. There was no pressure at college, but he had been home for a few weeks now and he was regretting it. He hadn't the money to go travelling with the lads and his parents hadn't the money to lend him. His summer job in the garage didn't pay much and left him with dirt under his fingernails that washing wouldn't shift. He had taken to digging it out with a galvanised nail at idle moments. His mother said it made her feel sick.

There was nothing for him in Bailey anymore and he couldn't wait to put it behind him. He'd miss Josh but not much else and he had told his younger brother often enough to get the hell out as soon as he could. He hoped he'd listened and be off to college, or travelling soon.

He'd better or he'd end up trapped in this good-for-nothing town.

Since he had gone away, Callum felt worse every time he came back to Bailey. There was something badly wrong with the place. It was like it had a bad smell that no one else could get. When he tried to talk to people about it, they just dismissed him. Bailey was fine, grand, no problem. Never mind that people died in accidents more often here than anywhere else. That was another reason he wanted his brother out. His parents were probably OK, but Josh noticed things. He'd notice soon enough about Bailey and then he'd be in trouble. *Danger*, Callum thought, then he'd be in danger.

He stepped out into the night. The weather had been great, but the night air still gave him a shiver. The moon was fat and the sky clear, stars like crystal chips. It was too dark to see the river but he could feel it there, not far from the house. He slipped out through the garden gate.

Old Doc Naylor had refused to talk about Bailey when he had tried to make him over the last couple of weeks, but Callum knew that he took night-time walks around Bailey and down by the river. If anyone knew anything about what was wrong in Bailey, it was Naylor. Callum would get it out of him tonight.

He walked along Abbey Street, named for some abbey that no longer existed. *Typical of this town, he thought, living in the past.* When he turned the corner into Sugar Lane, named for its old trade of storing sugar, he suddenly smelt the river. It was initially a fresh wet smell, with a hint of the exotic in it. He knew that the town had once been an important port for the import and export of spices and hides, animals and food. The smell of the river seemed crowded with the smells of the past. And there, underneath, was the scent of corruption. He thought he had imagined it before this, but now, in the night, there it was for real. He took an experimental deep breath through his nose and gagged. There was something dead in it. Lots of something dead.

He glanced back at Naylor's top-floor apartment in Abbey Street. There was a light in one of the windows. He watched for a while but there was no flicker of TV, no movement visible through the uncurtained window. He continued down Sugar Lane until he met the quay and crossed to the boardwalk. The river was there beneath him, dark silk hiding God knows what in its depths. He walked upriver, keeping the water on his left.

The moon made everything easy to see. At the far end of the boardwalk, most of the length of the town away from him, he saw a figure looking into the water. It was most likely to be Naylor. Callum walked on, not hurrying. He didn't want to intimidate the man. Callum was big and Naylor, though tall, was scrawny and wary.

He needn't have bothered. Naylor didn't notice he was there until he spoke.

'Hey, Doc.'

The man's whole body jerked. 'You. You gave me a scare.'

'Sorry.'

'What are you doing out here?'

'Taking a walk, same as you,' Callum said.

Naylor shook his head. 'You followed me. You want to talk about ... things.'

Callum stepped close to him. 'You know what I want.'

'Yes, and if you knew what you were asking, you wouldn't. Just go back to college and forget about Bailey.'

'I can't do that. I have a kid brother.'

Naylor looked at him. 'We all had someone once. Better off without.'

Callum gripped his elbow, this time standing tall and letting his size intimidate. The man's arm seemed nothing but bone.

'I'm not like you. I want to protect him. Just tell me what I need to know.'

Naylor looked at him. 'You already know what you need to know about Bailey. Now, let me go, if you won't go yourself.'

Naylor shook his arm and Callum let him go, although the urge to physically force the man to tell him was strong. Naylor walked away, followed by a long moon-shadow.

Callum swore and turned to look at the river. There, where Naylor had been looking, he noticed a curious eddy in the water. It looked like a constant series of ripples as though a fish was touching its mouth to the surface over and over. The effect was of a small vortex in the otherwise smooth silk of the river.

He took a step closer to the edge of the boardwalk and stopped himself.

'Don't stand too close, Cal, you idiot,' he said under his breath.

He took a step back but felt the bulk of another person behind him. He swore and turned around fast. No one.

The bad feeling started to come over him again and the smell of the river rose to his nostrils, a brown smell, made up of mud and sediment and the unending flow of water from the mountains. But this time it didn't smell bad. It smelt enticing. He turned back towards it. The water really did look like silk. Quite inviting. He had always liked to swim. It was sensual, even sexy to be in the water. The girl he was seeing in Dublin liked to swim with him, her body wet against his.

It was really lovely in the water. He stepped closer and leaned, just a bit. Dark silk that would wrap around him like a woman's body. All he had to do was just slip in.

The chill that he had felt earlier under the clear sky was gone. Now, he could feel real heat in the night. Sweat popped out on his skin. He couldn't bear it. So sticky and unpleasant. The water would be delicious.

'Yes,' he said and slipped off the boardwalk.

Chapter Two

'Richard, are you all right?'

His wife was sitting beside him on the sofa with her hand on his arm.

'You drifted off. You were having a nightmare.'

'I'm OK. What time is it?'

She checked her phone. 'Nearly nine. '

Richard sat up. 'Do you want anything, Lynn?'

'No, thanks, love. I might go to bed if you don't mind.'

Richard smiled at her and put his hand on her bump for a second. She covered his hand with hers and smiled back.

'OK, I'll be up in a while,' he said.

Lynn pottered about, getting ready, giving him a kiss before she went upstairs.

When he was sure that she would be asleep, Richard

got up and walked around, feeling restless. The house was really clean and tidy and Lynn's hospital bag was packed. Everything was ready. The house was easy to keep up anyway once they'd got everything in its place. It still smelt new, of timber and carpet. As he passed the kitchen window, he saw the dustbin. He had to remember to put that out for collection in the morning.

He put the kettle on although he didn't really want tea. While he was waiting he went and looked out through the French windows at the back patio which overlooked the river. It was still bright enough to see the water. It was always there, always. It was the main reason they had bought the house, but he didn't like it anymore. He shuddered.

A rook landed on the railing of the patio and Richard marvelled at it. It should have been roosting with its fellows for the evening. It was huge this close. Its beak was grey and fierce. It looked at him, its shining black eye glittering with intelligence. Richard moved back a little from the window. The bird hopped along and leaned forward, keeping its eye on him. He came close to the window again and waved his hand at it. It didn't move.

He rapped the window. '*Get off!*'

The bird ruffled its feathers and flexed its body, releasing a huge wet stream of droppings onto the railing. It stood there casually for another second, staring at him, before it opened its wings and took off. It flew close to the window, then swerved upwards and went out of sight.

The kettle clicked off and the sound made him jump.

He was so tired. He hadn't been sleeping well lately. The practice was still new to him and, thanks mostly to the good offices of the practice's old secretary Dolores, he had kept a lot of the old doctor's patients. He was busy all day, with a steady stream of summer colds, colicky babies, high blood pressures and the multifarious ailments seen by a small-town general practitioner. Plus, with the baby coming there was a lot to think about.

He was so sweaty – even now, in the evening. In this spell of hot weather, he had started to take an extra shirt to work with him to change into in the afternoon. His back got hotter and wetter against the leather of his chair as the day wore on.

He made a cup of tea but one sip just made him feel like he was burning up. He longed for cool air. The moment he thought it, nothing else would do. He shoved his feet into his sneakers and went out the patio doors, ignoring the mess the rook had left. The garden beyond was open to the river, something he would have to rectify before the baby was mobile.

He set off walking upriver and the breeze was lovely.

Soon, he reached the town and walked along the boardwalk. There were people ahead, two of them, but he paid them no attention. When he glanced at them again, there was one, then a moment later none. He didn't know where they had gone but didn't care. He didn't want to talk to anyone, he just wanted to walk in the cool air next to the river. As he passed the spot where they had been, the water was disturbed. They must have thrown something in.

The further he got from home, the darker the night became and the harder Richard found it to think about work, or Lynn and the baby. His mind seemed fuzzy. It was easier just to walk and watch the river. A bat was hunting, catching bugs over the water. He saw fish jumping as if there was something after them.

He rounded one corner and stopped. There was something standing on the path in front of him. It looked like a large dog. It turned red eyes on him and he felt a shiver of fear. But it turned its gaze away and slipped into the tangled undergrowth beside the path.

Richard started walking again, keeping close to the river as he passed the place where the dog had gone. He walked on, forgetting the animal. He had a headache and felt so tired. He really should turn back, but his feet just kept moving in the same direction. He shook his head, trying to dislodge the buzzing. He couldn't think straight. It was that damn dream again. It started to come back to him in the darkness. There was something about the river and some woman with brown hair. He remembered running. He shook his head again.

He came around another bend in the river and saw the lockkeeper's cottage. He stopped and stared at it. There was something about it. He couldn't take his eyes off it. His head began to pound and he could feel his heartbeat in all his pulse points. He went away from himself and when he swam back to awareness, he was standing next to the window.

What are you doing? Richard, what the hell are you doing?

But he kept on standing there. After a while, his chin dropped down to his chest and he almost dozed. His head came up when he heard a huge splash in the river. He turned, feeling like he was moving in soft tar. He saw the glint of eyes in the river before a thick body rose and fell, curving like a snake. When it disappeared, he realised that his headache had broken, leaving him feeling weak and grateful.

He walked back along the riverbank, keeping his head down, watching where he placed his feet in the darkness.

He got back to the house and turned on all the lights. He stood in the kitchen and leaned on the breakfast bar. The night lay outside the French windows but he could only see his own reflection. His glasses made him look like he had no eyes. It came to him that anything could be out there on the river, just looking at him. He crossed the kitchen in three big steps and jerked all the curtains closed. He pulled at them until even the tiniest gap was covered.

He went up to bed but just lay there beside Lynn. He was afraid to go to sleep. He didn't want to dream.

Chapter Three

The evening had grown dark and by the time Kate finished cleaning up after her dinner, the night had begun to press itself against the window panes. In the silence of the empty cottage, she heard an enormous splash from the river, followed by a low gurgling sound. She locked all the windows and drew the curtains. As she closed the ones over the sink, something scraped against the glass and she shrank away from it. She had a bad feeling that there was someone out there, watching her. She sat on the sofa and put a noisy quiz show on the TV, cranking up the sound and concentrating on the questions. If the thing in the river moved again, she didn't hear it and all was quiet when she went up to bed.

She checked the bank-account app on her phone. She was being careful with the money, and paying the bills that her mother used to. There was very little money coming in, but there were some savings. The craft market had taken some of her paintings and three had sold so far, which was exciting and put some cash back into the coffers. She thought she would be OK until her mother got out. She just hoped it would be soon.

The daytime was fine. She kept herself busy gathering sticks for winter in case she was still on her own, and painting, and tidying the house. She stayed away from the river. She was only seventeen, but she was young, not stupid.

She called out goodnight to her mother, although she was miles away in the hospital, drowsy from anxiety tablets. The sound of her voice in the empty cottage, unanswered, made her shiver. Sleep soon claimed her though and the dream came again, starting the same as always.

She was asleep in bed until a noise woke her. She got up and made her way down the hall in the dark. Her bare toes curled on the carpet and she hugged herself against the cold. She pushed open the front door and walked across the wet grass to the edge of the river.

The river was black, starless eternal night. She wavered on her feet and felt a sickening vertigo seize her. She felt herself swept up and out over the water. She could barely see as she was spun in rapid circles. She felt an intense cold wrapped around her. Her arms were pinned to her sides and her nightdress whipped around her legs. She tried to cry out for help but she couldn't open her mouth. She couldn't breathe.

She was spun across the water and slammed into the river, hitting its hard surface with a slap. It opened to her and she was in, and under. She opened her mouth to scream and tasted the bitter brackish river on her tongue. She was still being spun, blinded by the dark water and the force of her movement. She clamped her mouth shut and made one tremendous effort. She succeeded in thrusting her arms outwards, finding her voice at the same time. Some word escaped her in a stream of bubbles, some word she didn't understand herself. At once, she was released and left turning slowly in the water, not knowing which way was up in the dark.

She woke and stared at the darkness. The cottage was deeply silent, a soundless vacuum waiting for something to come. She cleared her throat to break the deep sink of emptiness but the sound echoed against the blankness. She had an impression of the universe flying away from her.

She had to pee. She had a cold moment of fear when putting her feet out onto the floor. The silence had an alive feel to it, a suspended moment. When the edge of her slipper touched her foot, it felt like a finger. She bit her lip hard. If she screamed into that silence, she might not be able to stop. She almost ran from the bedroom into the hall. There was moonlight from the skylight.

Why didn't you turn on the light, Kate?

She blinked. Why hadn't she turned on the light? That was the trick to banishing night fears. Turn on the light, check under the bed and in the wardrobe. It's what her mother had done when she had nightmares as a child. Put the light on, prove there was nothing to be afraid of.

Except her mother wasn't here anymore. And Kate wasn't so sure that if she looked under the bed she wouldn't find anything there.

It's not fair. I'm only seventeen.

She shook her head, making her hair fly. Seventeen or not, she wasn't about to start saying things weren't fair. If she did, she might cry and crying in the empty cottage might start something she couldn't stop.

She shuddered and the urgency in her bladder got her moving.

She went into the bathroom and peed. When she stood up, she saw herself in the mirror. Her curls were tangled. Her skin was OK but she had dark rings under her eyes. She blew her nose on a piece of toilet paper and turned to throw it into the bowl but stopped, her hand raised. The water was black and thick with mud. As she watched, the shape of a face bulged out of the glutinous mess, its eyes open.

'*Katie.*' The gurgling voice was full of muck and illness, but was unmistakably her father's voice.

The face firmed up as she realised who it was and some of the black mud fell away.

'*Kate. Kate. Come to me, Katie.*'

Kate tried to say no, but her voice had gone.

'*Katherine. I'm your father. Obey me.*' The voice was thicker and angry.

'No,' Kate said.

Despite herself, tears blinded her for a moment and she swiped them away. The face surged upwards, black teeth snapping. She fell backwards and ran from the room, pulling the door shut behind her.

She heard a surge and a slap from the bathroom and ran for her bedroom. She locked the door behind her and leapt into bed. She pulled the cover up to her neck and sat with her knees drawn up. She thought of the knives in the block in the kitchen. Even with the light on in the bedroom, the dark space under the bed was too ... full.

Sounds began to flood back in. She felt as though she was hearing more clearly than she ever had, so focused was she. Outside, night birds called in alarm and doves awoke and struggled to fly free of the branches, making crashing sounds in the dark. On the far bank, a fox cried its eerie call to the moon and was answered by a vixen in the woods. Eventually silence fell again.

The river continued on, emptying itself into the sea and sucking more life from the land, every day one of countless thousands.

Nothing came to her door and eventually she fell asleep.

She woke early in a crooked position. She wriggled her legs in the bed to wake them up and braved putting them out onto the floor, although she took a giant step away from the bed. She threw open the curtains and let the sunshine stream in.

She needed the bathroom but used the one

downstairs. She got ready and had a slice of toast with tea before going back to the upstairs bathroom.

She stood at the door for a long time before she was able to open it. There was black mud spattered on the floor. She walked over to the toilet. The water in the bowl was clear again, but there was a muddy handprint on the seat. She slammed the lid down on it and backed out of the room, shutting the door behind her. She thought briefly of calling Gabe to help her clean up, but knew she wouldn't. He was a great friend, her only one really, but this was her problem. She would deal with it herself. Or try to.

She gathered cleaning materials from under the kitchen sink and went back to the bathroom. She took a deep breath and got on with it.

Afterwards, she threw out the gloves she had used and scrubbed her hands.

Then she continued with her first ever commissioned painting. The picture was of Mrs. Salter's prize Cavalier King Charles Spaniel, Gladiator. Mrs. Salter was crazy about her dogs but certainly had a sense of humour about their names. Gladiator, or Gladys for short, was the softest, laziest dog Kate had ever met. The dog had no problem keeping still for the reference photographs Kate had taken. He just had a problem keeping his eyes open. Mrs. Salter either didn't know what age Kate was, or didn't care, plus she had money and other dogs. Kate was making sure to do a good job on Gladiator.

When she was satisfied with what she had done and was waiting for it to dry, Kate fetched her mother's scrapbooks from the locked cupboard under the stairs. Settled at the kitchen table, she put the books beside her and opened the first of the sequence.

The books were filled with newspaper clippings. Her mother had never let her look too closely at them, but had herself often pored over them. This was the first time that Kate had taken them out herself. She flipped the heavy pages, headlines flashing, dates written in her mother's neat cursive writing above each article.

21st June, 2001

BOAT LOST IN STORM, 5 DEAD
The longest day of the year brought with it unusual weather. A storm of terrible proportions destroyed several pleasure craft on the river, the sudden rise of the storm causing one to crash against the supports of Ó Murchú Bridge. All five of the people aboard perished in the tragedy. The body of the boat's owner, Nicholas O'Neill, has still not been recovered.

31st January, 2008

BODY FOUND IN WELL
The body of Jason Ffrench (42) a factory worker, has been discovered at the bottom of a disused well near the old town dump. The well was a narrow one and it is a mystery to police how Mr. Ffrench's body fell to the bottom. They are

calling for any witnesses to unusual activity in the area.

She looked at this one for a while. This was Gabe's father. That was a big thing she had in common with her friend. Both their fathers were gone. They didn't talk about it, but it was there.

28th April, 2012

GIRLS FOUND DEAD ON RIVERBANK
Twin girls Gillian and Patricia Murphy, aged 12, were found dead yesterday morning on the bank of a backwater of the river by a man walking his dog. The gruesome discovery brings to an end a week of searching for the little girls. Their distraught parents Frank (36), an accountant, and Patricia (34), a secretary, have been asking questions about how the girls could have disappeared from school without anyone noticing. They also want the police to explain how the girls' bodies were found in a place that had already been searched some days earlier.

She had known the twins. They had been a year younger than her, but she had been to their parties many times. They were the first dead people she had known, at least of her own age. Gabe's father had been a big man who she saw sometimes but not as often as Gabe's mother. And he was a parent, and so once removed from her. She and Gabe hadn't been best friends when he died, at least not like now. Now, she would be lost without him.

7th November, 2018

LOCAL MAN LOST – BODY STILL NOT FOUND

Kate had skipped a number of pages. Her father had gone out into the night and never came back. There were signs of a struggle on the riverbank and one single shoe left behind. They had dragged the river while Kate and her mother stood on the bridge, watching, hour after hour.

The article had appeared two weeks later and her mother had clipped it and spent a long time putting it in the scrapbook. Kate made her go to bed. After a week of her staying in bed and barely eating, Kate got the doctor. He had made the arrangements. Kate had lied to him about relatives being able to keep an eye on her. He had studied her for a while, but he was old and she had always found him cold. He shrugged and left and then it was just her.

She finished the school year by herself and kept her head down. The town left her alone for the most part. In fact, if it wasn't for Gabe, days would have gone by without her talking to anyone.

That first night, after her mother had been taken away, Kate had come out of the cottage and sat on the lock gate, looking into the water with dusk falling around her, bats flitting about and the last of the light gilding the river. She saw the first of the bodies without realising what it was. When she saw its destroyed face, she scrambled back onto the towpath and stared. It was joined by hundreds of floating bodies, rising from the water, their bones peach-coloured in the trailing sunset. They covered the surface of the river all around the lock. She backed away from the edge and they started to move, turning their faces towards her. She ran from them into the cottage and huddled on the sofa, her fingers clenched in the wool of one of her father's old sweaters.

She had nowhere else to go. Besides, running away only put things off. In the end, everyone had to come home, wherever that home turned out to be.

Kate put the books away and suddenly felt cold in the kitchen, despite the sun streaming in. She went outside to feel heat on her bare arms and legs. The river was beautiful, full of dancing light. She walked close to the bank and looked in.

Chapter Four

They found Callum caught under a dock downriver. Josh was in a search party that included his father when the news came that the body had been found. His father's phone rang and after a few minutes his whole body swayed from the knees. He took a step back, regained his balance and turned to Josh.

Josh didn't need to be told that his brother was found and lost all at once. His own legs turned to water and he sat down hard. He heard underwater voices shimmering around him and raised his head to see his father's hand and white face. He took the hand and rose. They each put an arm around the other's waist and walked like that the whole way home.

It was funny how that first phone call was followed by silence. He looked at his father's face, his mother looked at both their faces, everyone just knew. The time of no news when his older brother was missing was terrible and this time of the worst news was also terrible. The waiting had been unbearable but now there was no more hope left in the world.

Josh started towards his room but sat halfway up the stairs with no energy to go any further. He sat and listened to his parents' silence, an agonised breathing where the grief was too big to shed. The grief had got caught inside them, tangled like Callum had been under the dock.

The day of the funeral was the day Josh turned seventeen. His parents either didn't remember or didn't know what to do about it. His brother's coffin was solid and real. In comparison, a date in the calendar meant nothing. He said nothing to his parents.

After the burial, there were sandwiches and drinks. Josh told his mother that he was going for a walk. She nodded and shook hands with someone, her eyes glazed. He left the pub and stood on top of the hill, looking down at the river.

There was nowhere in town that you weren't aware of it. It was wide and full of channels and currents, brown, restless and always, *always* there. He couldn't avoid it, so he went towards it.

Reaching the quay, he turned upstream and walked until he realised he had left the boardwalk and was walking on the towpath. He looked back and the town was gone, hidden by a bend in the path. Ahead was the wood with its towering trees that fringed the river banks. The path was well worn and in danger of being taken over by the bushes that encroached on it and the undergrowth that wanted to creep onto it. On its other side the grass of the river bank was eating into it in parts.

He shuddered as he passed through a deep shadow that covered another curve. A heron scraped its rough prehistoric call, making him jump. One flew, making a rattle of reeds. It flapped slowly out over the river, its long legs dangling, its flight awkward. For one crazy moment, in the still heat of the river valley, the creature did look prehistoric – a pteranodon flying on leather wings, looking for prey.

'Shut up,' he whispered to himself. He was freaking out.

The sound of a whisper in the strange stillness that followed the bird's flight made him feel weird.

He cleared his throat and spoke into the heavy air.

'My brother is dead.'

As an experiment, he didn't think it had helped. It sounded like someone else had spoken. He stepped onto the bank and looked down at the brown water.

'My brother is dead, you bastard river!'

He looked around and found a big rock. It took two hands to lift it but he swung it into the water. It fell with a loud slap and created a wave. He watched the ripples fade. He had left no impression on the water. He wanted badly to do something, to hurt something, to burst the abscess of pain inside him.

He took a deep breath, threw his head back and let a roar come out of him. It rose to a scream and when he ran out of breath he collapsed on the river bank and tears finally came.

He cried, mostly silently, till his chest was hitching. He was glad no one had come because he wouldn't have been able to stop. He wiped his face with his hands and looked at his legs sticking out over the bank. He was wearing his only suit, brought out for weddings and other family occasions. It probably had grass stains on it. He lay back on the bank and squinted into the bright sky. When his eyes adjusted, he watched the clouds, clean, blameless shapes drifting above him. Dogs, horses, faces, fish, snakes ...

He closed his eyes and drifted too.

Callum was pulling his foot. He groaned and pulled his leg away.

'Stop, I'm asleep.'

His brother took a firmer grip on his ankle and pulled.

'Hey, stop, man!'

He opened his eyes. The clouds were moving and the grass was slipping from under his back. He got an elbow under him and saw the river coming closer.

'Hey!'

Something had him. He tried to turn but his leg was firmly caught. He scrabbled at the grass and tore out chunks, but it was too late. He was over the edge. The river came up around his shoulders and his face was suddenly under the surface. Despite the warmth of the day, the water was cold. It rushed into his mouth, brackish and choking. He blew it out in bubbles but he was still being drawn deeper. It was hard to see in the water, but he kicked down with his free foot, feeling his shoe strike something. He bent double and reached for his ankle where something was biting into him. His hands touched fingers which began to move. The hands crawled up his leg and in the dim brown light he could see arms and the beginning of a face.

'No.' He spoke the word underwater and the face smiled at him, ruined, awful and familiar. Loved.

Callum swarmed up his body until they were face to face. Callum's eyes were gone. When he leaned in, to kiss or to bite, Josh screamed with the last of his breath.

He opened his eyes to the clouds and sat up with a strangled cry. He was on the riverbank. Something slapped the water close to the bank. He scrambled to his feet and took one big step backwards onto the towpath. When the sound came again, he walked fast, blindly, upstream.

He rounded a bend in the path. He had reached the lockkeeper's cottage.

A tall girl about his age was on the towpath, looking at the water. She wasn't close enough to be sure, but he thought he recognised her. Kate something. She was standing still, her chestnut hair in a thick curly ponytail. She seemed to be entirely focused on the river.

A man was approaching her from the other side. He was staring at her too. Josh slowed. The hairs on the back of his neck stood up.

The girl didn't look up as the man moved behind her and stopped. Then he put his hands firmly on her back

27

and pushed. Without making a sound, she flew out and crashed head first into the water.

The man ran back in the direction from which he had come.

Josh ran for the bank where she had gone in, kicked his shoes off, threw his jacket on the ground and dived in after her. There was nothing in his mind as he dived, only the thought that he had to save her. When he hit the water, everything changed. His dream came flooding back. His body was arrowing down through the water but he was looking for Callum, filled with both fear and the maddening hope that he would see his brother again. He kicked sideways in time to avoid something large and jagged. A wrecked boat. As he turned he saw a trail of heavy liquid in the water. Blood. It cleared his mind. She was down here and bleeding. He kicked and twisted, trying to see her before he had to surface for air. With his lungs bursting, he exploded out of the water, snatched a breath and forced himself back down. The river fought him, pushing back against his full lungs, trying to make him float. He grabbed the edge of the boat and pulled himself down.

There she was, her hair and clothes floating. She was caught. *Caught like Callum, trapped in the river.*

He kicked and pulled his way to her, ripped her shirt free from the jagged metal holding her and swam to the surface, his arm around her waist. He made his way awkwardly to the bank and found a hand there reaching to pull them in.

The hand belonged to a tall kid with huge shoulders.

On the bank, he shoved Josh aside and turned the girl on her side. He thumped her back and she coughed water onto the grass.

Josh got to his knees. The big guy helped the girl to sit up and she looked dazedly at them, her eyes red-rimmed and bright green.

'Are you OK?' Josh asked.

The big guy scowled at him. 'Kate? What happened? Did this guy ...?'

'Hey, man, I pulled her out. Some other guy pushed her in. He ran off that way. I didn't get a good look at him. You know, what with jumping in the river and all.'

The guy was probably only his age too, like the girl, but he was fully muscled, bigger than a lot of adults Josh knew, a bit bigger than Callum even. His face was tanned and hard.

'Gabe, I'm fine. Someone pushed me and I banged my head.' She raised a hand to carefully touch her hairline. She took her fingers away and looked at them.

They all did. Blood.

'*Ugh*,' she said and Josh watched her face pale.

'You should go and rest and drink tea or something," he said. 'We should call the cops.'

Kate and Gabe glanced at each other.

'Gabe, help me up, please. I'll go inside.'

Gabe, who looked like he could lift both of them with one hand, helped her gently to her feet and they started off towards the cottage that was set back behind the path against a wall of woodland.

She stopped after a few steps.

'Are you coming?' she asked Josh.

He raised his eyebrows, ignored Gabe's scowl and, scooping up his shoes and jacket, followed them into the cottage.

Kate pulled a black tracksuit from a pile in a laundry basket waiting to be folded. Hers, he reckoned. She showed him to a small downstairs bathroom, which had a shower cubicle, to get washed and changed. There was a blue shower gel so he washed hair and body with that and was glad to rinse the brackish smell of the river off him. The tracksuit was too short in the leg but Kate was tall so it wasn't too bad a fit. When he came back to the kitchen, there was evidence that someone had mopped the wet footprints from the floor and Kate had washed and changed as well.

She was holding a cloth to her head and Gabe was busying himself making tea. Josh took a seat to her right at the table and they sat for a long while with no sound except the water starting to boil.

'Are your parents at work?' Josh said.

Kate shook her head and winced. 'No, it's just me here now."

'I don't understand. What do you mean, just you?'

'I –'

'Who are you anyway?' Gabe interrupted, giving her a look.

'I'm Josh Ryan.' He looked at the girl. 'Your name is Kate, right? You guys are in St. Joseph's?'

She nodded, more carefully this time. 'Kate Lynch. This is Gabe Ffrench.'

'Kate,' Gabe said, 'how do we know this guy isn't lying? Maybe he *is* the one who pushed you in.'

Kate looked at Josh, her sharp eyes making him uncomfortable.

'I don't think so. What are you doing out here anyway, Josh?'

Josh didn't know what he meant to say, but it wasn't what came out.

'It's my birthday today and we just finished burying my brother.'

Kate and Gabe shared another glance.

'Callum Ryan. Died in the river,' Gabe said quietly.

Josh nodded, his throat suddenly aching, He swallowed. The kettle came to the boil.

'I'm sorry,' Kate said. 'My dad died that way too. A few months ago. And Gabe's dad years ago.'

Josh nodded. He was used to hearing that from people. It had just meant nothing to him before. Now he knew how it felt.

'My parents are still at the afters. I couldn't stand staying there.'

Gabe took the cloth from Kate and rinsed it in cold water before giving it back to her. She smiled at him and pressed it to the wound. It had almost stopped bleeding but her forehead was already starting to bruise.

Gabe made them all tea and put a packet of cheap biscuits on the table. Josh helped himself to three. He suddenly felt ravenous and couldn't remember if he had eaten anything that day.

'Your mam will want to call the cops when she hears,

I'd say,' Josh said, hoping Kate would make clear what she had said earlier about it being just her.

Kate sighed deeply and drank some tea before speaking.

'She's not coming home. Not soon anyway. She's ... not well.'

'Oh,' Josh said. 'Sorry. Who lives here with you then?' He looked at Gabe, who was scowling again.

'No one.'

'What?'

'No one lives with me,' she said.

'Wait, you live here on your own? What are you – sixteen?'

'Seventeen.'

Josh looked from Kate to Gabe and back again.

'That's weird,' he said.

Gabe spoke gruffly, as though against his will. 'You don't know the half of it.'

Josh looked at Kate. She was tall and slender, almost thin. Her thick hair and her lovely eyes were the strongest things about her. When she looked at him, she seemed ready for a fight, but the natural shape of her lips was upturned. He wondered what she looked like when she really smiled. He caught flashes of strong white teeth as she talked. She finished saying something to Gabe and turned those flashing eyes on him, full of something he couldn't decipher.

'Have you dreamed about your brother yet?'

Callum's eyes. Josh nearly dropped his mug.

'Or seen him?' Gabe said.

Their faces were serious. Suddenly Josh felt like the oldest person in the room. They looked like lost children.

'What do you mean, seen him?'

'Have you seen him in the river?' Gabe said.

'That's – that's mean. Callum is dead, man.'

'We know. It's just that you might … see him again, is all.'

'What the hell are you saying that for? You're crazy.' Josh stood up sharply, tilting the chair, almost toppling it.

'Maybe, but that doesn't mean you won't see him. Just be ready when you do,' Gabe said.

'And remember that we're here,' said Kate.

She stood and held out her hand for him to shake. He took it reluctantly. Her skin was cold, despite the hot mug of tea, but she held on to him firmly.

'Thanks for saving me. Come back if you need to.'

'I'll drop back your stuff. Bye.'

Josh shoved his feet into his shoes and grabbed his jacket and wet things. The hall seemed very long and they followed him slowly towards the front door. He wrenched it open harder than he had intended and it banged against the wall. Across the towpath, something splashed in the river.

Josh looked towards it and saw movement. Faces in the growing twilight; faces rising to face the cottage. Callum's among them, his eyes missing.

Gabe reached a large hand out and slammed the door shut. Josh turned back towards them and caught a glimpse of his face in the hall mirror. Young, serious, terrified. Just like theirs.

Chapter Five

'What the hell?'

'Come back to the kitchen.'

'Did you put something in my tea?'

Kate put her hand on his arm. 'Josh, it's not us. It's ...'

'It's Bailey,' Gabe said.

Josh didn't want to go back to the kitchen but he didn't want to go out the front door either. He was suddenly stuck in this hallway with two people he didn't know ... and outside ... he didn't know what was outside.

'What the hell, man? What's going on?'

'Our dads were out there too. And everyone who's died in the river. Ever, as far as we can tell.' Kate's voice held a tremor. She cleared her throat and looked at Gabe, who sighed.

'Come on, we'll explain,' he said. 'Looks like you're in now.'

In the kitchen Josh sat down with them, but this time he sat closer to the back door. If they got any more crazy, he was going. Gabe was big, but Josh reckoned he was faster.

'See,' Kate said, 'there's something wrong with Bailey. With the river. Maybe the woods too.'

'And, because of your brother, now you know about it,' Gabe said.

'Although I think most people know something,' Kate said, 'even though they don't say or do anything about it. Once my father died, my mother couldn't bear seeing him and she had a sort of breakdown.'

'That's another thing,' said Josh. 'How come you're allowed to stay here on your own? Shouldn't you be somewhere? With relatives or, I dunno, the State or something?'

'Probably, but Bailey doesn't care. I kept going to school up to the summer and no one paid me any attention.'

'My mother keeps busy with book clubs and sewing groups and stuff – she doesn't notice if I come here a lot,' Gabe said, a look of defiance in his eyes.

'So, what are you saying? People die somehow in the river and then haunt it?' Josh said.

'Something like that.'

'Crazy. Look, I'm going home. My parents need me.'

Gabe shrugged. 'Go if you want. We don't need you.'

Kate stood when he did, but this time she didn't take his hand.

'Just be careful, Josh. Stay away from the river and wells.'

Gabe stood up too, his size making the kitchen feel small.

'And don't tell your folks any of this if you want them to stay safe. You don't want to draw attention to them.'

'Attention from what?'

'We don't know,' Kate said, her voice quiet. 'We don't know.'

Josh left by the back door this time, skirting the family car which was dotted with fallen blossoms from the tall trees. Kate and Gabe watched him go.

They stood at the door, breathing in the warm evening air and the scent of flowers from the strip of garden between the house and the sudden rise of the woods.

Although they weren't touching, she could feel warmth from Gabe's shoulder, close to hers.

He had been such a good friend to her for the last few months. She knew he wanted to date her, but that seemed impossible. She was in a holding pattern, waiting for her mother to come home. And, besides, he was her friend. She knew she loved him, but not in the way he wanted her to. She sighed and leaned against the side of the door.

'Kate.'

She looked up.

He didn't wait for her to speak but pulled her into his arms. It felt good to be held and he was warm and strong. She didn't pull away when he kissed her but she couldn't kiss him back. He finally stopped, resting his forehead against hers. Kate felt tears spring to her eyes. She hadn't had a boyfriend yet and Gabe was the first boy to kiss her. She felt something but it didn't feel like she thought it would. She wanted to put her arms around him again, but was afraid that he would get the wrong idea.

He held still against her, his fresh breath tickling her skin. Then he straightened up and touched her cheek.

'Goodnight, Kate.'

'Goodnight, Gabe.'

He fetched his bike from behind the house and cycled towards the darkening towpath in a show of bravery.

Kate hurried back along the hall to the front door to watch him out of sight. Bailey was within walking distance, but that bend in the river cut her off. Loneliness swept through her and she wrapped her arms around herself. There was a thick squelching sound from the riverbank. The tide was low, leaving a shallow run of water over stones and mud and dead trees. She slammed the door and slid the locks across.

Chapter Six

Adam and the redhead left the club somewhere after two a.m. The exit led down a slope to the street and he tucked his arm around her waist to protect her on the slippery cobbles. Once they turned the corner, he pressed her against the wall and kissed her.

'*Get a room!*' someone shouted.

Adam grinned against her mouth. She giggled.

He caught her hand and ran with her down the street. She turned her ankle on her high-heeled shoe at the end of the street and pulled him to a stop.

'I can't run. Walk me home?'

Adam had been looking for a likely doorway, but she wanted to go home. Still she had pressed against him willingly enough and she was a looker. Maybe he could spare the effort to walk her home. There might be other opportunities along the way.

'Where do you live then?' he said, putting his arm around her waist.

'It's in the country a bit. It's scary going home by myself.'

Adam rolled his eyes. She had better oblige him if he had to walk into the sticks and back again on his own. When they left the town behind and the road was lit only by moonlight, he stopped and turned her towards him, kissing her hard.

He pulled away and started looking for somewhere to go. The broken rafters of an old house showed against the moonlight and he pulled her towards it.

'No, not there, it's scary.'

Adam pushed through the open doorway, brushing aside some branches. He pulled her after him and looked around. There was a little tree growing from the floor but otherwise it looked pretty good, not wet or scummy and no rats that he could see.

'I don't like it here,' she said, her voice starting to whine.

'Maybe you'll like this.'

Adam pulled her close and kissed her again. She seemed to forget her concerns and sank down when he pushed her.

He lay down beside her. 'Here, swallow this.' He pushed a tablet into her mouth. Her forehead furrowed but she swallowed when he took one as well.

He moved a little to get more comfortable and then leant over her.

But she wasn't looking at him. She was staring over

his shoulder. He felt a flash of rage. He should slap her face. That would get her attention.

'Hey. What are you doing?' He gave her a sharp poke in the ribs, holding himself up on one arm. The feel of her flesh giving beneath his finger and her wince of pain excited him. But still she hadn't looked at him.

He twisted his neck to see what was so fascinating that she couldn't pay attention to him. He saw something move in the rafters of the rotten roof, just a flicker of moonlight. Then he focused harder and saw a bone-white face staring at him. The eyes were yellow slits and white hair hung around the face. Adam's teeth clenched and he bit his tongue. Blood washed into his mouth and he turned and spat. For a second he was absorbed by the dark spittle which had hit the girl on the bare neck. Then he heard a scream above him, an inhuman shriek that filled his head and made his teeth clench together again. He rolled away from the redhead and struggled to his feet.

His ears were ringing and he couldn't hear the sounds of the night.

The girl just lay there, her limbs slack.

'Get up, you retard!' Adam hissed.

The face in the roof screamed again and Adam fell to his knees, hands over his ears. He felt wetness on his palms. The pain was unbearable and, while he couldn't hear the sound anymore, the waves of it washed over him and he rolled forward and cracked his forehead on the broken floor flags.

Everything went black and when he came around,

feeling sick and dizzy, he heard a car pass and felt a wash of relief that his ears still worked.

'What the hell was that thing?'

Adam sat up slowly and looked over at the redhead. She was lying in the same position. Adam got up and went over to her, still feeling dizzy. He poked her with his foot and she didn't move. He stepped over her and got down to look at her face. Her eyes were open but clouded over, opaque.

Adam shoved himself backwards, scrabbling to stand up. He burst through the branches crossing the doorway and ran for town.

Chapter Seven

Richard was looking at the scalpel. It was beautiful. A wonderful piece of steel, perfect, the right weight, fitting into his hand comfortably. He rotated his wrist, admiring how it gleamed. He touched it to the pad of his thumb, watching as a drop of blood welled up and held there, bulbous and pregnant. He swayed his thumb from side to side and watched as the dark-red bubble burst and ran down his thumb onto his wrist. He put his thumb in his mouth and sucked it clean. Then he ran his tongue over the streak going down to his wrist. He looked at the scalpel and saw the tiny drop of blood on its pointed tip. It fascinated him. He brought it close to his face and looked at it, one of his eyes closed to focus on it. The thought came to him that he could put it into his eye. The headache might be in there behind it. He could dig it out. He brought it very close to his eye then took it away. It was meant for something else. He put it back in its sheath.

His vision blurred red as if he had sliced his eyes.

He had been carrying the knife since Saturday. Lynn had gone for a lie-down. Richard had thought he might go for a walk. He went upstairs with her and pressed a kiss to her forehead, letting his hand slip under his pillow as he did. She hadn't found the scalpel because he had straightened the bed that morning. It was hard for her to bend over. He slipped it into his pocket as she turned over to take her nap. He shut the door and went downstairs.

He left immediately on his walk and headed towards town. He walked quickly through the town and beyond, and soon he was near the lockkeeper's cottage. He continued on past it, then he hid in bushes at the side of the towpath, fingering the scalpel in his pocket. His headache was back.

Sometime later – he didn't know how long – he stepped out on the towpath again. He walked back to the cottage.

The girl *(only a girl)* came out and stood on the towpath, looking at the river. Richard pulled out the scalpel. He unsheathed it and put the cover back in his pocket. He palmed the scalpel and walked forward quickly. He stepped behind her. She didn't look around at him.

A powerful beat of his headache blinded him and when he opened his eyes again, he saw the sunshine on her chestnut hair and the movement of her breath in her body. The urge in him was too strong to deny. He raised both hands, the scalpel palmed in one, and pushed her as hard as he could. She was slender and, taken by surprise, she seemed to fly from his hands far out over the water before she crashed back down into it.

Someone was coming towards him. Richard turned and ran back in the direction from which he had come. He was going farther from home, but he just wanted to get away. His skin was cut and bleeding from palming the scalpel. His headache had broken and he couldn't quite believe what he had done. He ran for a long time. Why had he done that? He couldn't remember.

He still sometimes felt like he had never reached home at all. But he slid his hand under the pillow again and felt the scalpel. It made him feel safe enough to close his eyes and shut out the light.

Chapter Eight

Alma bent over and leaned on her knees. Her pulse was thundering all over her body. She thought she might have a heart attack. She heard voices coming close so she stood up and began walking, her chest burning with the effort of not panting. The women passed her. Shorts-wearing, tanned and above all skinny women, chatting as they walked. Alma hated them and felt bad for it. But it was the least pleasure she could get now that she was denying herself all other pleasures. She couldn't eat anything nice and this was the first of regular walks that were supposed to be saving her life. When she dropped dead, they would find a big fat girl with mousey hair and a cheap tracksuit. She had considered dying her hair, but that would just make her a big fat girl with brassy hair. She let her breath heave in and out and she got dizzy with the rush of oxygen. That last hill was a killer. She couldn't face it anymore. She'd finish her walk on the towpath.

Alma had a dread of rats but the river path was long and flat. She'd risk seeing a rat for a bit of steady flat ground. She took a shortcut across a green and went as fast as she could through the streets, not wanting to look at the pretty people strolling in the evening sunshine.

She reached the towpath and started along it. The breeze coming off the river was nice and the murmur of the water was like soft voices. There was a festival on in town tonight, so the path was deserted. She slowed down and began to enjoy herself a little bit. The birds were singing and a soft dew made her feel cool. The feeling of the evening drawing in gave her a sweet melancholy that she found satisfactory. She ambled along, pulling wild flowers from the bank and shredding them. The rosy light on the river was sort of hypnotic.

She knew that the lockkeeper's cottage was coming up soon. She would go as far as that, without getting close enough for anyone there to see her, and then she would head back.

She rounded the corner and saw the cottage. Someone was coming out the back door. She stepped off the path and dragged herself up into the woods where she sat on a fallen log. It was pleasant in the dim light. Everything smelt mossy. She knew that her face was probably still all red and she smelt sweaty.

There was some conversation from the house. She peered through the branches and saw them. Two young men and that Kate girl from school. Kate was tall and slim, delicate really. She had long curly brown hair. It wasn't fair. Alma focussed on the boys. Just boys, although one of them was huge. She recognised him as a boy who had been in a lot of trouble at school. She switched her gaze to the other one and her breath stopped in her throat. He was beautiful. He looked around once and his eyes were really blue and the whites really white. His face was perfect. He had all those things that she read about, chiselled jaw and cheekbones, straight nose, sensual lips. His body was lean and the T-shirt pulled against his chest as he moved. She moaned a bit from her hiding place and leaned out to look at him. She definitely didn't know him. No one could forget a face like that. Alma sat back and settled into herself like a cloud.

Two boys. Kate had two, one big and good-looking, the other lean and beautiful. And she was skinny and pretty. It just wasn't fair. Alma didn't have anything and that Kate got to have everything, even a pretty cottage by the river. It was totally unfair. She dug her fingers into the soft wood and felt woodlice and spiders running over her hands.

When the boys left, the big one pushing his bike, Kate went into the house, Alma stood up. She slipped and stumbled down the slope and stepped back onto the path, glad of the firm footing. She stood there getting her breath back and then walked over to the cottage as if it were her own. She ran her hand over the warm stone wall, leaving clots of dirt. She went up the garden path to the front door. She rested her face against it, still warm from the day's sunlight. She scratched her dirty fingernails down the wood.

'You inside. You with everything. It's not fair,' she whispered. 'Not fair at all.'

She turned and went back down the path

'Not fair at all! Not fair at all!' She sang it like a mantra all the way home in the darkness.

Chapter Nine

Captain Halley pushed open the doors of the tavern and the smell of roasting meat, sweating men and stale beer assailed his senses. The heat wrapped itself around him though and he was grateful for it. They had been away from home for a long time on this trip and the men had unloaded the cargo and beaten him to town before he finished his business on the quayside. The port was as busy as usual and he had hailed a few of his fellows before following his men across the quay to town and the promise of food, drink and a steady bed, and maybe a girl to share it with. He was tired and felt much older than his forty years.

He let the door swing shut behind him and heard a roistering shout from the spot nearest the roaring fire. His men awaited him. They had all earned good wages on this voyage and got on pretty well with each other for a group of uneducated men trapped together on a small ship. They didn't seem to hold his education against him and some of them even let him teach them how to read. At the beginning of the voyage, he had looked quite different to them. He hadn't worn a beard and his brown hair was well groomed. He was brown from the sun, but not as weather-beaten as his crew. Despite his best efforts while at sea, he looked more like their kin now, with a thick beard and overlong hair.

They welcomed him now with the good nature of men full of food and drink, warming their cold damp toes in front of a fine fire. A few of the serving girls were young and pretty and glad to have new blood in the port by the looks of them. It promised to be a grand evening.

Halley allowed himself to be taken into the group and accepted the plate of food shoved into his hand. He drank a pot of ale before he started on the grub. He felt like he hadn't eaten in a year.

When he finished he sat back against the hard bench and ran his hand over his bearded face. He scratched at his chin and hailed one of the girls, shouting to her that he wanted a bath. She laughed at him and swayed away, speaking into the ear of the landlady. They might laugh at him, but there'd be a bath of hot water upstairs when he wanted it. He had stayed here before when he was in Bailey and a little extra payment got him the extra service that made him feel like a gentleman again.

Tomorrow, when he was clean and rested, he'd go and search out his old friend for a long talk. Halley was from Glendalough in Wicklow, the same village as the abbot of the monastery here. Nicholas and he had wrestled as boys in the hills of Wicklow and chased women together as young men in

Dublin. But Halley heard the call of the sea while Nicholas heard God's call. Funny how they should both end up in Bailey, not that Halley was ever long in port. It would be good to see Nicholas again.

Halley had got used to Bailey and the townsfolk seemed to like him. He always tried to be fair and it had got around. Sometimes, the men took advantage of it, but only a little. Besides, he'd rather they liked him than feared him. He saw that other ships made plenty of money through running the men on fear, but his ship did well enough. In the long run, he might be doing better because he kept the same men year after year and they were loyal to him. Any cheating was only done by themselves. They wouldn't stand for any other man cheating him.

Halley yawned, feeling the bones of his jaw creak. He would stay by the fire for another hour to let the landlady heat the water for his bath, then he would go. He wanted to shave himself and have a girl visit him before he collapsed into sleep. He was looking forward to it and to his meeting with Nicholas on the morrow.

He waved to a friend of his from a different ship and the man came over.

'Halley, you're back, you bastard. How are you?

Barron was a great bear of a man and when he cuffed Halley on the shoulder he was knocked into the sailor next to him, spilling a bit of his ale. The sailor looked around at his captain and grinned a gappy grin at him before turning back to his mates.

Halley shouted to Barron to sit down and the big man picked up a sailor and tossed him into the crowd where his mates laughed and threw him back onto a different bench. Barron sat in the narrow space he had made, squashing Halley and overwhelming him with the scent of whale grease and rum.

'Ha' ye heard about the toll, man?'

Josh woke up, the question echoing in his head. *'Ha' ye heard about the toll, man?'* He stared around his bedroom, not recognising anything. The scent of the river came to him on the night air and he remembered. He scrubbed at his face and lay back down. It had been the most vivid dream of his life.

He put his arms behind his head and stared at the ceiling. The image of Kate's face filled his mind. He drifted to sleep and, this time, he dreamt of green eyes.

Chapter Ten

In the morning, Josh dressed in his normal clothes of jeans and T-shirt and went downstairs. His parents were drinking coffee in silence. He took Kate's clothes from the drier and put them in a gym bag. He sat for a few minutes with his mam and dad but no one was saying anything.

'I'm going to the gym. Will you guys be OK?'

His mother looked at him with red eyes. Her face was slack, her skin grey. They both looked old.

'Be careful.'

It was something she had always said when he and Callum were leaving the house but, this time, it seemed invested with a greater weight. He opened his mouth to say something but Gabe's words came back to him. *And don't tell your folks any of this if you want them to stay safe.*

'OK, Mam, I will,' was all he said.

He gave each of them a kiss on the forehead before he left. His father closed his eyes and gripped his coffee mug.

Alma got up early and showered. She stood in front of the mirror afterwards and looked at herself. She grabbed her belly fat and rolled it, manipulating it like dough. She had been walking every day since Saturday and not having anything nice at all. She went back into the bathroom and stood on the scales. No difference. She got down and walked back out to the bedroom. It just wasn't fair. She looked at herself again, then closed her eyes. She pictured the young man behind her, putting his hands under her arms, pressing himself against her, his lean hard chest hot against her skin. He touched his hot mouth to her neck and she shuddered. Every part of her was aware of him. When she opened her eyes, she wasn't sure whether she had been dreaming of him or imagining him. All she knew was that she felt cold without him.

She poked through her clothes but everything was the same. Long dresses in dull colours. She picked a dark green one and pulled it on. When she sat down for breakfast, she vowed that she wouldn't think about him again.

But he was so beautiful and it was so unfair.

Her mother was eating already, stuffing her mouth with Danish pastries. Alma looked at her, disgusted. But she was hungry and, after a brief internal struggle, she reached out for one of the glossy cakes. They ate in silence together.

After breakfast, she headed out into the sun, pulling her sunglasses down from her hair to cover her eyes. It was another lovely day, the kind of day that made it bad to be fat. Her legs got sweaty and rubbed together, starting another rash. She hated the summer. It was easier to cover up in the winter. All the slim girls were dashing about in little skirts and shorts. Alma didn't own anything that made her look nice, or summery. She didn't look in the shop windows because her reflection was always there to mock her. She felt drab and heavy and sick with despair because she had eaten the pastries for breakfast. But it just seemed so pointless when she had so much weight to lose. What difference would a pastry or two make?

She picked up what she needed from the shop and went to sit down on a bench on the quay. Lots of people had ice-cream cones. She wanted one. She had just about made up her mind to get one (what difference would it make?) when she saw the young guy coming towards her. She froze in a sort of terror. He looked like he was going to sit beside her but instead he stopped and leaned on the railing to look into the river. He stayed there a long time and she drank him in. He was wearing jeans and a T-shirt and leaning on the railing made the shirt pull up and show his lower back. Safe behind her sunglasses, she started to relax. His legs were long and lean, his shoulders broad but not overblown. He was delicious.

He stayed at the rail for another few minutes before checking his watch and walking away. Alma followed him. Watching his easy loping movement and the flex of lean muscle under his T-shirt, she wished more than ever that she was skinny. He went into the music shop and she followed, pretending to examine some CDs while watching him in the instrument section. He sat down at a piano and put his fingers on the keys. He sat there for a minute, then played a couple of fast scales. He paused, his fingers still touching the keys, then started to play a piece of classical music that Alma recognised but wasn't able to name. She moved away from the racks of music and went to stand where she could see his face. He had his eyes closed and his hands were moving magically over the keys. Alma stared at his face, rapt. He was expressionless as he played, except sometimes his eyebrows moved.

A few other customers paused in their shopping to listen to him. A woman asked what he was playing and someone answered, 'Fauré's Pavane.' Alma repeated it to herself. She wouldn't forget. It was beautiful and so was he. All she wanted to do was touch him, to go over there and put her hands on his shoulders and have him smile up at her. He finished playing and put his hands on his thighs. A smattering of applause broke out. He jerked and looked around, his face flushing. He ducked his head and moved away from the piano. Alma hung around, lifting things and putting them back, not seeing what she was looking at.

She turned away as he left the shop. She thought he looked at her and her heart pounded as if he had unexpectedly touched her. She dumped the book of music she had been holding and left the shop. He was taller than most people on the street and her gaze fell on him straight away. She followed him to the quay but couldn't keep up with him. That was OK. She knew where he was going.

A man crossed her line of sight and she looked at him. It was the new young doctor. He stared at her, unsmiling, frowning a little. She recognised the look in his eyes. He stared at her long enough for him to have to twist his neck to look back at her as he walked. Before he turned away, he nodded to her and she nodded back. They were the same. Maybe she would go to see him later, but first she wanted to be where the boy was.

Josh had pottered around town for a while, trying to relax. He spent some time in the music shop. It was his favourite place. The manager didn't mind if he played the piano a little. People liked when he played. Callum had liked it too, had often told him that he should get further training and be a music teacher. It seemed too big to think about now. But the music was nice. Sometimes it helped him to think and sometimes, like now, it helped him to stop thinking.

When he felt ready, he turned towards the river. At the edge of town, he hesitated between two paths. After a moment, he chose the towpath. It was the quickest way and he still thought that Kate and Gabe had worked themselves up because of what happened to their families. He wasn't exactly in his right mind after Callum's death himself. So he walked the towpath and made himself look at the river. Ahead, a rare kingfisher was diving on the water. Josh watched it for a while before the rhythm of movement lulled him into a restful state. It really was beautiful along the riverbank. He almost felt good, although his mind kept whispering to him that Callum was gone. Poor Callum, drowned in the brown water. He stopped for a minute to look at it. It was quite clear really. He could see fish darting and the more he looked, the more colours and life he saw in there.

It was cool and lovely. It would be nice to sit and dangle his feet in the silky water. He wasn't in any kind of hurry after all.

Callum is dead. Dead in the river, caught in old shopping trollies and fishing lines.

He brought his hand up and slapped himself in the face, hard. His head rocked sideways. Finding himself too close to the edge of the river, he stepped back hurriedly and walked on, this time keeping his eyes firmly on the path ahead.

He rounded the last bend and saw the cottage. It was a pretty cool house. The old lockkeeper's cottage had been extended, but in the same style and the same local stone. In the small gardens either side of the path to the front door was a profusion of flowers. People had cared about the place.

As he approached, the front door opened and Kate came out. Seeing her, after dreaming about her, took his breath away. The sun was in her hair, bringing red highlights out of the chestnut. At this slight distance, she looked like a young woman, troubled, but enjoying a moment of sunshine on her face.

His sneaker scuffed a stone and she opened her eyes. She smiled when she saw him and it lit her face as though the sunshine had got inside her. It was a smile that was impossible not to return. In that tiny moment, the sunshine on her lovely face was like sunshine on the water. Yesterday, he had thought her pretty. Today, with that smile, he saw that she was beautiful.

He raised the hand that had slapped his face and waved at her. Maybe she was crazy and maybe not, but all he knew was that he wanted to stand beside her and look at the light in her face.

'I brought your stuff back.'

'Thanks. Do you want some toast?'

In the same spirit of defiance that had brought him along the towpath, they had tea and toast at a white wrought-iron picnic table in the garden. Despite everything, they found things to laugh about.

Alma walked along the towpath, not minding when a rat dropped into the water ahead of her. She was too busy thinking. Her hands were squeezing the fat of her belly, squeezing and releasing, squeezing and releasing as she walked. Her breath became short but she felt full of a burning energy. It made her feel like her body was humming. It was like being turned on by something inappropriate or eating a whole cake in secret. It sort of felt bad, but exciting at the same time. She reached the cottage without remembering the journey.

She stood, screened by bushes, and watched,

picturing their cosy little scene inside.

Then they came out and settled down at the wrought-iron table with tea and toast.

She watched, now calm and in control of her emotions.

The girl was the only thing in the way. And she was skinny. She wouldn't put up much of a fight.

She walked away, knowing what she had to do.

Gabe slammed his fist into the punchbag. He was sweaty and exhausted. He hadn't slept well. He never did after he saw his father in the river. And after kissing Kate, he couldn't think of much else. He would never want to do anything to hurt her. He wished it had been him who had pulled her from the river yesterday. It wouldn't have been the first time.

He took down the little photograph of her that he had tucked into the mirror. Her lovely face was serious in the picture and she was engrained on his heart. She belonged to him even if she didn't know it yet. She owned his heart entirely. He just wanted to be close to her. Nothing else mattered. Maybe Josh was OK, but he hoped he wouldn't come back. He was too good-looking in his suit, even soaked from the river. He didn't want him hanging around Kate.

He tucked the picture back into the mirror frame and went to have a shower. He got under the hot water and began to soap the sweat from his body. He scrubbed his face and shampooed his short hair. When he was clean, he stood under the spray with his eyes closed, letting the water rush over his face. The water felt hot and heavy on his skin and he licked his lips. It tasted brackish and like iron to him. There must be some mineral in the water supply. In fact, it smelt a bit rusty too. The water began to spurt and sputter and fall more slowly. Gabe stepped out of the main surge and wiped his hand over his eyes. When he opened his eyes he thought he was cut. There was blood all over his hand. He looked down and saw streaks and lumps of it running into the drain. He turned around and saw that the shower itself was spraying blood all over the cubicle and all over him. He yelled and banged the door open, falling over the step onto the bathroom floor. The shower continued to spray blood but it was now clotting in the drain and escaping onto the floor. He used his foot to slam the shower door shut and scrambled to his feet. He caught sight of himself in the mirror as he got out of the room. He was covered in blood and there were lumps caught in his short hair. He stood in the hall looking at his bloody footprints. After a minute, the sound of the shower changed to a more normal spray and he went back in. He opened the shower door and saw that the water had returned and was washing the blood away. He shut the door again and let the shower run. He got into the bath and used the short hose on the taps to clean the blood off. The water was cold and it took a long time to get it all off. By the time he was finished, he was numb. He got out and wrapped himself in a robe. The shower was still running. He turned it off quickly and left the bathroom.

He sat on the bed and looked at his phone. She

would want to know but it wasn't something he could put in a text. He was going straight there.

Kate and Josh were at the picnic table outside the cottage when Gabe arrived on his bike. His face tightened when he saw them together but he said nothing. Instead, he leaned his bike against the house and sat down with them.

Keeping his eyes on Kate, he told his story about the blood in the shower. Kate put her hand on his for a second, before tucking both hands out of sight under the table.

'Do you want to hear more, Josh?' she said.

Josh looked at their faces. Even Gabe waited to hear his answer. They looked eager to tell their stories. Maybe they were crazy but something about them accepting him, wondering if he would accept them, was appealing. He was lonely. For the moment, it felt good to be with people who were talking to him. He took a deep breath.

'On the way here, I wanted to get into the river. I slapped myself in the face.'

The others looked at each other and Gabe nodded.

'My father disappeared a few months ago,' Kate said. 'The river took him. But there was other stuff before that. When I was five, I got scarlet fever and had to be in hospital for a while. It seems I was delirious. I don't remember any of it, but my mother told me that I was raving about the river. From then on I sometimes saw things that most other people didn't notice. I heard screams in the night that my mother told me was the banshee. You saved me from the river yesterday, Josh, but it wasn't the first time I nearly drowned. On my seventh birthday, I was waiting for my party to start. I was a bit cross because I couldn't run around in my party dress. I was in the garden, sulking a bit, kicking things.'

Josh smiled at the thought of the young Kate raising hell and accidentally caught Gabe's eye. They looked away from each other quickly.

Kate closed her eyes.

Her mother said she could change into jeans after the food and everyone could play in the garden. Right now, she was wearing a pink-and-white dress with white socks and pink shoes. She had sat on her bed in the morning and admired those shoes, turning her ankles left and right. Now, she just wanted her wellies so that she could wade in the shallow part of the stream and look for frogs. She went to the edge of the stream where it widened into a pool and looked down. She knew it was deep because her dad had shown her how far down he could poke a long stick into it. A frog flashed across just under the surface. She saw his legs kicking out.

It was a sunny day, but under the overhanging branches it was cool and dark. Kate edged a bit closer and grasped a branch to lean in and look for the frog. Her skirt rose a little in the back as a breeze caught it. She heard a dog begin to howl at a neighbour's house and then the wind really came up. It swung her forward and she only barely held on to her branch, using both hands. The toes of her pink shoes were still on the

63

bank and she tried to pull herself around to get her weight back over them. The wind whistled around again in a vortex and flung her out over the pond. She held the branch but heard it crack above her head.

She tried to make a leap to the opposite bank but crashed down into the pond, going under the cold water. She gulped a breath before the fast current running under the pond sucked her deep and her legs went under a heavy fallen branch. She lay face down on the bottom of the pond, her legs stuck and the current inching her further under the bough. Her hands had disappeared into the mud. She saw the frog swim past her eyes in the murk and began to struggle in earnest. As she moved, the mud sucked at her and she went into it until she was up to her elbows in the dark sludge. Bubbles escaped her mouth and her lungs were going to burst. She scrabbled for purchase but at first the mud seemed bottomless. Then she touched something that gave under her fingers and looked down. Her scratching hands had uncovered a face in the mud and her nails had left gouges in its cheeks. She screamed underwater, losing the last of her breath. The eyes in the face opened. The white mouth laughed and a stream of bubbles surged out into the water.

Her vision filled with black spots which started to close in. She felt a sudden sharp pain in her scalp as her floating hair caught on something and she was pulled upwards. With the last of her strength she pushed off the bough as her legs came free and she cleared the surface.

A boy changed his grip on her hair to grab at her arm. He heaved her up onto the bank and she flopped there. He thumped at her back until she coughed water up and was sick *on the grass. She rolled away from it and the boy helped her sit up.*

'You were wearing black jeans and a *Star Wars* T-shirt and you had mud all over them.' Kate looked up at Gabe, smiling.

'I was.' He smiled back.

Kate looked at Josh. 'I saw the face again on Friday in the toilet upstairs. It changed to look like my father. He spoke to me. I know it wasn't him though. It was the river.'

'Or whatever is in it,' Gabe said.

'Then,' Kate said, 'a few months ago, my parents had a row and I heard my dad say he wasn't going to take it anymore. He ran out of the house and by the time my mam and me followed him, he was gone. They didn't find him. I thought when they were searching for your brother that they might find Dad too, but he's really gone.'

'Could he have just left town?' Josh said, with an apologetic grimace.

She frowned at him. 'He wouldn't do that to us. Besides, they found some of his stuff in the water. Just not him.'

'Sorry.'

'It was too much for Mam. The old doctor committed her but she wanted to go. The hospital is inland. I think that's better for her.'

She looked at them both, her green eyes suddenly fierce.

'My dad tried to fight it. It killed him but he was

right to try. I don't want to live like this. I want my mother to come home and for everything to be normal. I'll fight it on my own if I have to.'

'You won't have to,' Gabe said.

'I'll help you,' Josh said, at the same time.

They glared at each other.

A cloud covered the sun, leaving them in a sink of dead heat. There wasn't a breath of wind, but Kate suddenly pointed at the river.

There was a wind out there, dancing water-filled whirlwinds off the river. The surface rose and formed the shape of a great eel. It lunged towards them and broke against the towpath. A wave washed up almost to their feet, making them jump up. The water slid back towards the river, moving more slowly than it should have. Josh realised that Kate was between him and Gabe, holding their hands.

'I guess it knows we're on to it then,' he said.

Kate laughed, a slightly hysterical sound. Gabe grinned. They were together. For the moment, that was enough.

Chapter Eleven

'Ha' ye heard about the toll, man?'

Halley shook his head.

'It's your mate, the friar. He's charging a toll for all the ships to come up the river. You've been gone too long. There's going to be a war in this town if something isn't done. Will ye talk to him?'

'Who's asking me, Barron?'

Barron made a sweeping gesture with his great fist.

'The lot of 'em, boy. Someone has to talk sense into the man and we reckon you're the only one who can.'

Halley looked around. He noticed a lot of eyes on his exchange with Barron. The big man must have been deputised. The faces didn't turn away when he met their gaze. Instead, nearly all the men nodded to him, frowns and determination showing.

'How much is the toll, Barron?'

Barron said the figure, not taking his eyes off Halley.

Halley felt his face freeze despite the heat and the rum fumes being breathed on him. It was so much. What the hell was the man thinking?

'I'll go up to him in the morning. I'll talk to him. Tell them I'll talk to him.'

'You don't know all that's been going on here since you last sailed, Halley. It's been bad. Anyone who stood against him is dead.'

Halley shook his head. He didn't believe it.

'Go to see him. But just keep your knife about you.'

Halley stared into the big man's black eyes. There was no hint of joviality about him.

'I won't be harmed. Tell the captains I'll go at daybreak. I'll bring what news there is.'

Barron nodded and rose. Halley called for another drink and drank it back. He couldn't believe it. Barron must be wrong. He'd be at the abbey by dawn. He'd find out for himself.

Josh came awake and found himself sitting on the edge of the bed. This was the second night he had dreamed of the captain. He had never dreamed with anything like this level of detail before.

He went to the window for some air. A chill wind was rising through the town from the river. Below him in the garden, a dark shape like a large dog raised its head. Josh felt its red eyes upon him and tried to look away. The creature opened its mouth in a red laugh and disappeared into the shadows.

Josh pulled the curtains and lay on the bed. He knew he wasn't going back to sleep for a while. They needed information about the town. He googled it on his phone but there was only general touristy stuff. He dozed a little while waiting for it to be a reasonable time to text Kate.

Chapter Twelve

The library was a hexagonal building with huge windows built on a hill overlooking the lower town. Josh, Kate and Gabe trooped inside. It was almost deserted on such a warm day. It smelt of warm books and felt somnolent.

Only one librarian worked behind the counter and one man sat at a table, his chair turned to face the view.

The librarian looked up. 'Hi, Kate. Your book came in.' She took a book from the reserved piles to her right.

Kate handed her a library card and she checked the book out to her, and handed it over.

'Thanks, Rowena.' Kate stroked the cover of the book.

Josh looked over her shoulder. It was a book on growing vegetables.

'We're looking for information on Bailey's history,

Rowena,' said Kate. 'Have you got anything?'

'Local history, down the back. But you should talk to the Doc if that's what you're interested in.' She gestured towards the man sitting by the windows. 'He's read everything we have about Bailey.' She lowered her voice. 'And he likes to talk.'

Kate smiled and raised her eyebrows to Josh, who nodded.

They went through the sunlight to where the man sat with his face raised to soak in the heat.

'Excuse me,' Josh said.

The man squinted one eye open and examined Josh.

'The librarian said you might be able to help us. We're looking into Bailey's history.'

The man turned his head on his thin neck. 'Why would you want to do that?'

Josh didn't know how to answer. 'I just wanted to ask you a couple of questions. If it's not too much trouble?'

The man dragged his chair around and rested his elbows on the table. He wore a long scruffy grey ponytail and had a darker grey beard. He was very thin, with broad skinny shoulders that made him look hunched. His fingers and joints were filled with great round bones, looking like someone had stuffed marbles under his skin. The skin on some of his fingers looked hot and stretched. He pointed at the chairs and rested his dark stare on each of them in turn.

'Sit down and ask your questions.'

'Thank you. I'm Josh Ryan. This is Kate Lynch and Gabe Ffrench.'

The man looked sharply at Josh. 'Keith Naylor. Was Callum Ryan your brother?'

Josh nodded. Naylor looked at him for another moment before turning his gaze on the others.

'I've seen you in here before,' he said, nodding to Kate. He looked at Gabe. 'Not you, though.'

'I'm not much of a reader,' Gabe said.

At once, Naylor dismissed him and turned his attention back to Josh.

His eyes were a watery blue. 'Well, what do you want to know?'

'Are you from here, Doctor?' Josh asked.

'No. And I'm not a doctor.'

'I'm sorry. The librarian called you that.'

'People do. Everything is easier to deal with when it's catalogued. Makes it easier when you die too. I used to teach in Trinity College. English. The language of the invader, but I thought it a noble pursuit to fill the minds of young people with poetry and rhetoric. As it turns out, their minds were already too full of pop music and drugs to absorb anything else. But I know a little history too. The study of any subject is really the study of history.'

Naylor's eyes rolled in their cavernous sockets and settled on Kate.

'Do you intend to go to university, young woman?'

'I think so, yes, sir,' Kate said.

'To study or to have fun?'

Kate sat forward. 'Both, I hope.'

He sniffed and shrugged. 'As it happens, I've learned

more since I left the hallowed halls than I did there, so I won't lecture you.' He beetled his brows and squinted his eyes at them. 'So, questions then.'

'Could you describe Bailey to us? What do you know of the town?' Josh said.

Naylor was silent for a long moment.

'Describe Bailey, eh?' He sucked his cheek and stared at Josh. 'It was built by Isabella, the daughter of the Norman invader Strongbow, and her husband William Marshall, as a walled town. The current bridge is the seventh one. '

'They taught us that in school, Mr. Naylor. We were looking for some real stuff. About the real town.'

Naylor was still.

'I know what you're looking for. The same thing your brother was looking for. Why do young people always think they can change things? You can't change anything.' He glared at Josh. 'Do you want to end up like your brother?' He looked at Kate and Gabe. 'Or your fathers? Oh, I know who you are. You're not the first youngsters to come to me, poking their nose in where it doesn't belong. Don't you know that's the way to make it come for you?'

'Make what come for us?' Josh leaned forward.

'I'm saying no more.' Naylor folded his hands together on the table and leaned back. But words were part of his soul. He leaned forward again. 'You children – you're like students interested in the occult. The best thing to know about Bailey is when to leave. And that time is now, when you're still able to.'

'Why are you safe?' Kate asked. 'You seem to know and nothing's happened to you.'

He glared at her. 'You don't know a thing about what's happened to me. You're just starting to find out what it means to live at the foot of a volcano. I've done it for years, suffering, surviving.'

'But you observe the volcano,' Josh said.

Naylor folded his fingers stiffly together. 'It would be foolish not to, wouldn't it?'

'Tell us and we'll leave you alone. We're already in trouble. What difference would it make?' Josh said.

Naylor raised his eyebrows and was silent so long that Josh thought he had clammed up completely.

Then he sighed. 'Not here.' He nodded towards the front desk. 'She listens.'

'Do you know somewhere we could go?'

'It seems you can't be put off. Perhaps I owe you something. I was the last to see your brother after all. We'd better go somewhere indoors. We don't want to be near the river.'

Josh felt the blood drain from his face. Naylor was the last to see Callum?

The old man got up without waiting for an answer and waved at the librarian before stalking out into the sunlight.

They followed him.

'Save your breath,' he said. 'We have a lot of stairs to climb.'

He led the way to a three-storey merchant house on Abbey Street. He used his key to let them into a communal hall. They began climbing an airless stairwell and eventually came out on the top floor. Small windows in the hall showed a view of a church on one side and glimpses of the river on the other, glinting in the spaces between the lower houses.

Naylor unlocked his door and they entered. The flat was entirely walled by books, except for the end looking over the roofs of the lower houses towards the river. That was made almost entirely of glass. An open door showed a hallway leading to the rest of the apartment. The place had deep-red wooden floors and two big soft couches that faced each other. There was a simple kitchen occupying a small space at one side of the open-plan apartment with a small breakfast bar enclosing it. It was unexpected and attractive. Josh had imagined the man living in squalor.

'It's lovely,' Kate said.

'Thank you,' Naylor said, looking around with satisfaction.

He went to a small fridge and poured glasses of Coke for them all. Josh could see that the fridge held little else. Naylor drank deeply and looked into his glass as if it held the best vintage.

'To Bailey's black heart!'

A tremendous crack was followed by flying glass as the back window of the flat crashed in. Everyone ducked and Josh tried to cover Kate. She was silent but he could feel tremors in her back. Gabe was separated from them by a table, but he was making his way to them, keeping his head down. Wind was sucking the broken glass around the room in a funnel. Most of it was above their heads but Josh felt some of it strike his back. Keeping his head down and his eyes shut, he pulled Kate closer. His back was freezing and his T-shirt had pulled up, leaving it more exposed, but he could feel Kate's warmth seeping into his front. Glass lashed at his hands but he kept them around Kate's head, protecting her scalp. The wind sounded like a guttural voice speaking in an unknown language. It roared and hissed around the apartment. Gabe made it to them and wrapped his big arms around them, helping Josh to cover Kate.

When the noise and wind stopped, Gabe stood up. Josh didn't move at first. His ears still hummed with the pressure of the sound. He opened his eyes and realised that nothing was moving around him. He got to his feet. Glass showered off him onto the floor. The apartment was ruined. Books were scattered everywhere and dishes had smashed onto the kitchen floor. Naylor was cowering under the kitchen table.

'Are you OK?' Josh asked Kate as he helped her up.

Kate nodded. He wasn't sure if she'd want it, but he put his arms around her again. She hesitated for a second and then hugged him. As she did, Josh became aware of multiple points of pain in his skin. The backs of his hands were bloody too.

Josh looked over to see Naylor crawling out from under the table. He didn't seem hurt.

Kate turned to Gabe and checked him. His T-shirt was heavier than theirs and he only had a few cuts.

Josh's stomach flipped as she ran her hands over Gabe's shoulders.

'Mr. Naylor, do you have anything that I could clean the cuts with?' she said.

Naylor blinked at her, his eyes seeming more cavernous than before.

'Of course. Of course. In the bathroom. I'll show you.' He went out of the room, walking like a much older man, his shoes crunching glass.

'C'mon, both of you. I want to make sure there's no glass in the cuts,' Kate said.'

The three of them followed Naylor into the hall. They waited while he rummaged in the bathroom cabinet. He brought back some supplies and bundled them into Kate's hands before standing there awkwardly, his big shoulders hunched.

'I'll make tea, shall I?' Naylor said. 'If I can find cups.' Without waiting for an answer, he nodded to himself and stalked away.

In the bathroom, Kate cleaned their visible cuts first, then when she was satisfied she looked up at them.

'You'll have to take your shirts off.'

Josh felt a little heat creep into his cheeks. They could hear the sound of glass being swept in the living area.

'You first, Gabe.'

Gabe pulled his shirt off with a look towards Josh. His body was as ripped as Josh had expected. He was tanned as well. He wasn't too badly cut and it didn't take long to clean him up. Josh tried not to look at Kate's hands moving over his skin. Then it was his turn. He took his shirt off, feeling glass pulling at him. He was fairly fit, but he couldn't compare with Gabe physically. His body was long and lean rather than heavily muscled. His face flamed and he was glad to turn his back. There was a long moment of silence before she picked up the tweezers and started picking glass out of his skin. It took a long time. When she finished, she soaked cotton balls in iodine and gently cleaned the wounds. Then he heard her ripping the plasters open. She applied some to the wounds.

'It's not too bad. Most of them are shallow and aren't bleeding anymore, so they don't need plasters,' she said. 'There are a couple of deeper ones. The worst one is down here.' She touched a fingertip close to the deepest wound on his lower back.

He shuddered slightly, feeling goosebumps rise on his skin.

She applied another plaster. 'Done,' she said.

Josh turned around and fingered his bloodied T-shirt.

'Think he'd have anything I could borrow?'

'Let's go see,' she said.

They trooped back to the main room and found that Naylor had swept all the glass into one big pile and was pouring dark tea into mismatched mugs.

'Help yourselves to milk and sugar. I have chocolate biscuits. Good for shock and all that.'

'Would you have a shirt I could borrow? This one isn't in good shape.'

Naylor took a blue shirt from his dryer. Josh put it on. It was a little big, but respectable. He sat down and Kate fixed his tea. He asked for no milk and one sugar but she gave him two heaped spoons. He took a sip and found the extra sweetness welcome. He swallowed a bite of chocolate biscuit with a second sip of tea.

'What the hell was that anyway?' Gabe asked.

'It was like the wind that knocked me into the pond when I was a child,' Kate said.

'Maybe now you could tell us what you know about Bailey, Mr. Naylor,' Kate said.

'You'd better call me Doc. Well, it seems like you might know as much as I do.'

He raised his mug and seemed about to toast again but thought better of it. He took a sip and put the mug down, touching his finger to the drip of tea on the side.

'There aren't any words for Bailey. It just is. People die here, but a lot of them live too. It's like there are two Baileys. In one, people work and eat and watch television and have babies. In the other, there are dark vibrations which can cross over. I've lived here a long time and I eventually noticed that there was a pattern about the crossovers. They used to happen about three times a year, not always the same times, but usually three. I always thought there was a collective sigh of relief when the third time had passed. If there was any of the year left, the town seemed to brighten up and things would be better. Even folk who saw nothing unusual were in better moods than normal at those times. But this year, things feel different. There are already three dead. Your father, your brother and there's that girl who was found in the ruined cottage. That's a lot for so early in the year. And then this, of course.' He gestured to the open space at the end of the apartment.

'Is there anything we can do about it?' Kate said.

Naylor shook his head. 'No one has been able to stop it for hundreds of years. I don't know what you think you can do.'

Josh looked at the others. Naylor was old and defeated. They would do something, which was more than most.

'You said you were the last to see my brother.'

Naylor's expression was hard to read. He nodded slowly.

'He was asking questions about the town too. I told him to get out. He said he couldn't while you were still here. I didn't see him again after that and a few days later I heard he was missing.'

Josh clamped his teeth together, trying to force a surge of pain back down his throat.

'I'd tell you the same except I suppose you can't just pack up and go at your age,' Naylor said. 'If you can't go, then you should at least stop asking questions. Don't draw attention to yourself.'

'Why are you talking to us when you wouldn't talk to Callum?' Josh said. 'Aren't you afraid of drawing that attention yourself? I mean, weren't you doing so before this happened?' He gestured to the broken window.

Naylor gave him a funny look, holding his gaze for too long.

'I don't know,' he said eventually. 'Maybe it's just time. But you still have a choice.'

'Yeah, and I'm making it. It's too late to stop,' Josh said. 'Whatever this is, it killed my brother and their fathers. I'm not stopping now.'

'Me neither,' Kate said.

Gabe kept his eyes on Kate. 'I'm in.'

A whistle of wind moved through the flat. It sounded like a distant voice answering a challenge.

Chapter Thirteen

After a thorough scrub and a shave, Halley whispered in the ear of the girl who had brought his hot shaving water and had lingered in his room after. She was the prettiest serving girl in the tavern and she smelt clean. He kissed her and her arms came around him. He felt like they were blended together. He looked at her with surprise and found the same expression on her face. Later, instead of urging her out of the room, he lay beside her. She tucked herself into his chest and they slept for a few hours in each other's arms. He awoke to moonlight in the room and her soft breath on his arm where it supported her head. She stirred and looked at him, stretching like a cat against his body.

She whispered to him that dawn would come soon and she had fires to set. He let her go and watched as she pulled on her red dress. She smiled at him as she left and he put his arms under his head and breathed deeply. He felt so good that he only rested for another minute before springing out of bed. He pulled on his clothes, wincing a little at the sour material covering his clean body.

He went quietly downstairs. There were still a few carousers who gave him a sleepy wave as he passed through the main room. Their faces were red with drink and the embers of the fire. Halley stepped out into the grey pre-dawn and took a deep breath of the cold air. The scent of the docks was on it and he could hear men talking to each other as they worked. The voices were in various tongues. Irish and English, but also French, Spanish and Italian voices were to be heard along the quay front. Halley could smell spices and the bloody scent of iron.

He turned left and began walking along the cobbled street. He turned up one of Bailey's many hills. He wanted to settle his thoughts before approaching the abbey. He saw its shape in Abbey Street but walked away from it. When he reached the top of the town, he proceeded along the town wall, passing its gates. The town was walled in a semicircle, bounded on the open side by the river. The true Irish lived outside the town, which was commanded by the Anglo-Normans. He passed the Maiden's Gate, and the Maiden's Tower, reserved for those who committed crimes against women. A voice hailed him from the tower as he passed but he ignored it. The houses were in darkness and silence still but smoke rose from their thatched roofs into the crisp air.

When Halley felt that he had reacquainted himself with the town that he thought of as home, if any place on land could be called that, he turned back towards the abbey.

He was approaching its walls when a figure stepped out.

In the middle of the night, Josh woke up, feeling stiff

and sore. The dream began to slip away but he got a scent of musk that brought an image of the girl in the moonlight. She had green eyes. He groaned and rubbed his face into the pillow. The room was too warm and stuffy. He got up and went to the window.

The moon was fat and he couldn't see anything moving out there. He realised that all the little hairs on his body were standing up. He looked out and where the garden should have been, and the street and the houses across the road, he saw the river. There were lights floating on the water. They were diffuse and rising and falling slightly on the slow waves. They floated closer to him and he squinted his eyes. One of them rolled to face him and he jerked back as he made out a man's face. He wasn't close enough to make out who it was, but he knew anyway. The other lights became clear. It was the moonlight shining on the faces of people floating in the water. As he watched, they began to struggle, their mouths open in silent screams. Their arms splashed the water as they began to sink. Water rushed over their luminous faces and flooded their eyes. There were hundreds of them, splashing and drowning. Eventually, they were all gone beneath the surface and the river was dark, except where the moonlight touched it.

Josh stood there, his hands clenched. The balls of light began to come from under the black water and rise to the surface again. The faces broke the skin of the water and their struggle started again. The closest one turned to face him and, this time, he could see that it had Kate's face, twisted with desperation and pain. Others rolled on the waves to face him and Josh saw Callum and Gabe. He felt their anguish and the bloody taste of anger filled his mouth. A dog began to bark somewhere in the dark.

The faces sank under the surface again and this time the water resolved itself into lawn, with dry flower beds that his mother didn't care about anymore. Josh heard a low chuckle under his window.

He gritted his teeth, shut the window despite the heat and went back to lie on the bed. His back hurt if he moved but it wasn't too bad. He lay in the dark, trying to control his breathing.

He heard scrabbling noises from the window and sat up. Although the window was closed, black, shining-wet river rats were streaming into the room. Before he could move, they were on him, the impact of their numbers knocking him onto his back. He swept them away but they were replaced immediately by a wave of others. He struggled and punched at them, but they clung to his T-shirt and his skin with their claws and teeth. The smell of mud and decay filled his nostrils. He could see their greasy fur up close, alive with fleas. He screamed as one of the rats squealed and bit into his neck. He smelt his own blood and heard his flesh tear. At once hundreds more leapt on top of the layers already covering him, squirming and squealing with excitement. He screamed again, emptying his lungs. They covered his face and he couldn't breathe. He struggled harder, feeling his lungs begin to strain. As

85

wave after wave covered him, he felt his chest unable to rise against their weight. Behind his closed eyelids, starbursts began to appear and he felt himself slipping away. As a tide of rats swarmed over his face, biting at his skin, he blacked out.

'Michael Halley, you're returned to us at last,' the familiar voice said.

'Nicholas Dunne, 'tis yourself,' Halley replied, smiling.

The abbot threw his arms around Halley and gave him a tremendous hug. Halley laughed when he got his breath back and clapped his old friend hard on the shoulder.

'Tell me about your travels, old friend,' the abbot said when they stepped back from each other. His staff with its distinctive cross on top was propped against the wall. His blue habit looked black in the night.

'I will, surely, Nicholas, but not now. I have to ask you a question.'

'You've been talking to Charlie Barron.'

Halley nodded. 'I have. And he's been telling me things I find hard to believe.'

'Then don't believe them.'

'But are they true, Nicholas?'

'Why must you talk about these matters of business, Michael? Come into the abbey and have something to eat.'

The abbot picked up his staff and turned to walk towards the gate of the abbey, but Halley stood his ground. He could see Nicholas's servant Long Pip standing at the gate. The dwarf was wrapped in a habit that was cut short but was still far too big for him. His small stature was made up for by his thick arms and chest. Halley had tried him at arm wrestling but had never succeeded.

'I'll have to know, Nicholas. If you're charging such a toll, then I'm to be charged as well.'

The abbot turned around.

'Not you, Michael.'

Halley closed the distance between them. 'I'm no different than the others.'

The abbot gripped Halley's arm. Halley was again aware of his incredible strength. He clenched his teeth together as the abbot's fingers dug into his bones.

'You are my friend, Michael, but heed me now. Stay out of my business, if you wish to remain so.'

'They look to me. You know they look to me. I can't stay out.' Halley shook himself free of the abbot's grip, but didn't step back.

Dawn was sending colour into the day and the abbot's green eyes were very bright in his ruddy face.

'And what are you going to do?'

'If this is all true, I'll have to oppose you. I'll have to.'

The abbot took a step forward, and spoke through his teeth. 'Think carefully on it, Michael.'

Halley shook his head. 'Has it come to this in Bailey, Nicholas? Do friendship and your vows mean nothing anymore?'

The abbot raised his hand to strike Halley but instead paused and patted his shoulder.

'Old friend, you will oppose me then?' The abbot's voice was sad.

Halley nodded slowly.

*'Then I will warn you to have a care, as you are now my
enemy.'*

Josh crashed out of bed, knocking his head against the
corner of the nightstand. He got to his feet and stared
around the room. There were no rats. The morning was
advanced and the sun hurt his eyes. He ran his hand
over his face and it came away with blood on it. He
went into the bathroom and looked at himself in the
mirror. Heavy stubble covered his jaw although he had
only shaved yesterday morning. He examined himself
closely but there were no bites anywhere on his body.
The blood was seeping from a cut on his head made by
the corner of the nightstand. There was no evidence at
all of the rats.

He showered and shaved and dressed in a green T-
shirt and jeans. Although the sun still hurt his eyes, it
wasn't as clear as it had been yesterday. The sun was
flashing in and out between scudding clouds. He looked
down and saw something on the timber floor of his
bedroom. He crouched down and tilted his head to get
the best angle. The timber was covered in tiny
footprints. Clawed footprints, hundreds of them. He
straightened up slowly and went downstairs.

He ate an apple and headed straight for Kate's
cottage. There was no thought in his mind of going
anywhere else.

The cottage looked welcoming. The doors and windows
were all open. He went round the back and rapped his
knuckles on the door as he stepped in.

Kate was gluing a blue flowerpot together at the table.

'Hi! Gabe's in the spare room having a rest. He didn't sleep last night. How are you feeling today?'

'I'm OK. I had weird dreams again. Very real.'

She nodded and he saw that she had shadows under her eyes.

'What do you think we should do today?' she asked.

'I think we should all get together with Doc Naylor and see if we can figure some stuff out. I think he'll tell us more. It's too late to stop now. This – whatever it is – doesn't want us knowing. All the more reason to, don't you think?'

'I do.' She went to the stairs. *'Gabe!'*

There was no answer.

She called again and listened. Nothing.

They went upstairs together but the room was empty.

Chapter Fourteen

He had heard them talking in the kitchen. He hadn't wanted to go there. He needed air without Josh breathing in it. Without him there watching Kate. He had slipped out and cut up through the woods.

There was no one about. He found a way through a thin covering of woodland into a field, ducking under barbed wire. There were horses visible in the distance. He saw a person in the corner of the field. A man who looked familiar.

The man beckoned to him so he walked towards him, looking down to make sure he didn't walk in manure in his sneakers. When he looked up again, the guy was gone, but there was a horse in the corner of the field, shadowed by trees. He stopped and narrowed his eyes, trying to find the man. The horse shuddered as if flies had landed on it. It rolled its eyes white and pawed the ground.

Gabe took a step back, feeling uneasy. He stepped into a pile of fresh horse dung and swore, looking at his sneaker. He heard a snort and looked up to see the horse racing towards him, all shiny black coat and white eyes. The hooves didn't seem to be making any noise on the soft turf, but its breath was snorting in and out. It sounded sick.

It came straight for him. Gabe knew he couldn't outrun the big animal, so he waited, intending to throw himself to one side and let it pass before running for the ditch. But the horse put its head down like a bull and seemed to sidestep with him. He turned to run away from it but felt a tremendous blow to his back. It felt like ice and burned him like extreme cold. Somehow, the horse had gone under him, feeling like the amorphous mud of the riverbank, shifting and changing shape as it needed to. He found himself on its back, facing out over its neck. It raced with him. He clutched its mane which was no longer shiny, but a straggly mass. He thought he felt something squirm against his fingers but couldn't look.

The horse turned its head to bite at him. He realised that its eyes were not rolling white as he had thought. They were just blank white with no pupil or colour. He had no skill in riding but his leg muscles gripped the animal's sides and his natural balance kept him on its back. He saw a huge hedge looming and he wanted to shut his eyes but couldn't. The horse rose in the air and cleared the obstacle. There was no impact as it reached the ground again. It raced on, faster than a horse should run. Gabe's fingers felt like they were sinking into its neck. He pushed hard with his elbow against its shoulder and felt the hardpacked muscle and bone give like jelly. Something black oozed out over his arm. The horse made a horrible screech but kept on its path.

Gabe looked up again to see the river. The horse was aiming straight for the mud and the water's edge. Gabe could see a gap in the fence. Not that this animal needed a gap. Gabe knew that it would try to drown him if it got him as far as the water. He braced himself and tried to fling himself from the creature's back. It was as if he was stuck in mud. Everywhere he touched the animal, it sucked at him and he couldn't escape it. He began to claw at it, tearing chunks of black mucky flesh off. He groaned in horror as his hands filled with the glutinous mess. He leaned into its neck and punched at its head. The face and eyes collapsed under his blows, but still it kept on running. Then it was through the gap and over a couple of feet of mud and into the river.

The deep channel that made the river navigable to ships wound close to the bank in places and the animal plunged straight down into it. Gabe was submerged but felt the flesh of the horse melt and disperse under him. He came gasping to the surface and struck out immediately for the shore. He wasn't a natural swimmer but again his muscles stood him in good stead. He used his arms and legs to propel him forward faster than he had ever managed before. All he knew was that he had to get out of the water. He felt something wrap itself around his ankle but he kicked at it with his other foot and knocked it away. He made the edge and hauled himself out onto the rock. Sitting on top of it, he looked at the river. He saw the horse's mutilated head roll out of the water. It became an eel, then its face changed to Kate's.

'Help me, help me, Gabe!'

'Go to hell!'

Immediately the face twisted into something black and weeping. It opened a huge maw and a bellow filled with the scent of decay and foul muck burst through the air to him like a giant bubble that broke against him, making his eardrums vibrate and his gorge rise. He turned and vomited onto the mud. It rose around his vomit and swallowed it into itself.

Gabe groaned and pushed himself to his feet. He walked wearily back to the cottage.

Chapter Fifteen

'Over the years, I've studied the history of Bailey as far back as I can,' Naylor said. 'Whatever this is, it has been going on a long time.'

Josh looked around at the others. Gabe, having showered and changed into a set of clothes that he kept in the spare room, had told his tale of the horse and Josh had reciprocated with his rats.

Following a half-pleading, half-demanding three-way conversation on the phone, Doc Naylor had turned up in an old Citroën 2CV, wearing loose black pants inside which his legs looked like blades. He had come to the back of the house and was now finishing his tea, having heard their stories.

'I can't find the reason for it, but I've amassed evidence of a lot of peculiar deaths and weird events similar to your experiences. Your story, Gabe, of the horse, sounds like a variation of the Púca, which is an animal spirit that takes people on nightmare rides. A lot of creatures that are told of in Irish lore have been seen in Bailey in relatively recent times. People in Bailey have reported hearing the Banshee, or seeing a fetch.'

'A fetch?' Kate said.

'A vision of a known person who is not really there.'

'You have a theory about it,' Josh said, seeing the gleam of the lecturer in Naylor's eye.

Naylor nodded. Now that they'd got him started, he had plenty to say.

'It seems to me that a few generations ago people all over the country experienced a lot more of the supernatural than we modern folk.' He leaned forward and looked at them all from under his heavy, untidy brows. 'It was commonplace for people to see ghosts or the will-o'-the-wisp, hear the Banshee or be afraid of fairies. Religion was an entrenched part of life. Now, *I* don't believe in God but it seemed to be a fact that if you did believe in one side of the spirit world, then it followed that you believed in the other. If you believed in angels, you believed in devils and all manner of other spirits. So if you thought it was not unusual to see a ghost, then there was nothing to stop you seeing one. In the modern world, however, people are more focussed on the material. They don't expect to see anything otherworldly. They have become closed off to anything outside their own experience. So, the supernatural is no longer commonplace.' He paused and unknotted his fingers to place his hands flat on the table. 'Except in Bailey. Here, the supernatural, the unusual, the weird has never been lost. These things are still commonplace. Strangers to the town don't see anything odd, because they are from places where the spirit world has become distant and those who are focussed on it are themselves considered strange. But here people live very close to the veil between this world and whatever else there might be. And I believe that the veil is thin and torn. I just don't know what has caused that to be the case.'

'So, we're seeing things because we're seeing them,' Gabe said.

'You could say that. I relate it to a woman who is breastfeeding. As long as the child keeps sucking, the milk keeps coming. For years, if it keeps going on. I think that Bailey is suckling on some sour teat and is growing more twisted with every suck.'

Kate made a face and Naylor cracked his knuckles.

'We need to find some way of breaking the connection between Bailey and the source of the trouble,' Naylor said.

Josh caught Kate's eye and she nodded almost imperceptibly. She obviously felt the same. Now, they only needed to figure out the source of the evil plaguing the town and how to defeat it. Simple.

Naylor helped himself to one of Kate's scones. He piled it with butter and jam and ate. The man was so bony he looked like he never ate.

'These dreams I'm having,' Josh said. 'They're following a sequence. I don't know how it's going to pan out but maybe it'll give me some idea of why this is all happening.'

'Dreams?' Naylor said, his eyes sharp.

Josh told him about the dreams and brought the others up to date.

'It might sound a bit mad, but I don't think they're dreams. I think they're memories,' he finished.

'Explain,' Naylor said.

Josh looked around at them all. 'I feel like I'm him. The captain. It's like it's happening to me. For a minute after I wake up, I feel ... different. I think we're connected in some way.'

'*Hmm* ... I wonder if you would be willing to try something?' Naylor said.

'Like what?

'Hypnosis. I'm not an expert by any means, but I could put you under to see if we can find out what's happening or why you're having these dreams.'

Josh raised his eyebrows. 'Put me under? What about bringing me back?'

'That as well of course. Don't worry, I'm quite good at it.'

Josh looked at Kate. She was biting her lip again. She did that when she was worried. It made him feel lighter to know that she was worried about him.

'Let's give it a try,' he said.

'Good lad.' Naylor rubbed his hands together, making a sound like sandpaper. 'Let's go to the couch. You should be comfortable.'

Josh followed Naylor to the living area and sat on the

97

couch. Naylor sat on the coffee table in front of him and looked into his eyes.

'Relax your shoulders and arms. Let them hang and rest where they are. Gradually feel a sense of relaxation spread from your toes all the way up your legs and into your body.'

Josh focussed on the sound of Naylor's voice. He did feel relaxed and sleepy. He suppressed a yawn. He hadn't got much sleep last night or lately. Naylor's voice droned on and Josh saw Kate yawn behind Naylor's back. It was enough to set him off and he yawned widely enough to make his jaw creak. His eyes watered and he laughed. Kate laughed too then Naylor raised his hands in a gesture of defeat but smiled a little too.

'Sorry, Doc, I guess it's not going to work. Maybe another time.'

Naylor nodded. 'It doesn't work for everyone, or at least not all the time. We'll just have to find out another way.'

Josh stood up and stretched.

'Let's provoke it,' he said.

'What?' Kate said.

'Let's make it mad. We might learn something. How about I go on the river?'

'No, you can't!' Kate said, standing up.

'Would you say that things have got worse?'

'Yes, since you started coming round,' Gabe said with force.

Kate gave him a reproachful look.

'Well, maybe there's something in that and the fact

that we're together now,' Josh said. 'Plus, I'm having the dreams or whatever they are. I'm going on the river.'

'Josh, please don't,' Kate said, coming over to touch his arm.

He frowned as he looked into her anxious face. 'We have to do something, right?'

Naylor spoke, settling himself into the cushions.

'Josh may be right. Confronting the – we'll call it evil for want of a better definition – might well bring us some vital information. I think it's worth a try.'

'I know we have to do something,' Kate said. 'It was me that said we have to do something in the first place. I just don't think that this is it. Too many people have died already.'

'Wait,' Gabe said. 'There may be a way.'

'Gabe, he can't go out there,' Kate said.

'Hear me out. So, some people in town don't seem to notice there's something wrong, and strangers never do, right? Tourists never do.'

'Go on,' Naylor said.

'So what if he goes on the river-cruise barge with a gang of tourists. That might act as a protection for him but maybe he'll get a feeling or have a memory or whatever. Maybe it doesn't have to just be when he's asleep.'

'It's a safer option, certainly,' Naylor said. 'Although not as likely to produce results.'

Kate glared at him before turning to Gabe.

'It's a good idea, Gabe. Except we're all going.'

'I think … I feel like it should be just me, Kate … I just feel it,' Josh said.

She frowned and shook her head. 'I don't care. We're not losing anyone else. We're trying it this way.'

'And if nothing happens?' Naylor said.

'Then we'll think of something else. But no one is going out there alone.' Kate's tone drew a line under the conversation.

In an odd moment of solidarity, Josh and Gabe shared a look. She had put her foot down and that was all there was to it.

Naylor wouldn't go. Even though he had been willing to send Josh on his own, he wouldn't listen to any argument about going himself. He held up his hands and would not be convinced.

Kate didn't care. She felt it was better with just the three of them. It felt right. They were going into this together and, despite the probable danger, she was upbeat. Doing something was always better than doing nothing.

Chapter Sixteen

The little booking office at the river-cruise barge had a queue. They shuffled along behind the rest but had to buy tickets for the next cruise as this one was booked out. They settled on a bench at the end of the bridge. There were plenty of people about. Josh went to the shop and came back with ice creams.

'Isn't this weird?' Kate said.

'Everything is weird,' Gabe said. 'Why this in particular?'

'Because it's nice. We're just hanging out, eating ice cream,' she said.

'That is weird.' Gabe grinned at her.

They fell into silence, concentrating on catching drips from the cones. Kate found herself watching the river. It held a fascination for her. She thought bodies of water probably did for everyone, but it was different in Bailey.

The river had ruined her life. It had killed her father, taken her mother from her and, before this was over, might very well have killed her and her friends. And yet, it looked so beautiful. Sun glitter was glinting off the tops of the little waves. The tidal nature of the river was unusual and she could smell a hint of salt, because the water was brackish. Seagulls were fighting over a crust of bread.

She finished her ice cream and closed her eyes. Her elbows were touching Josh on one side and Gabe on the other. Her mother used to say *'Left and right for the rats and mice, in the middle for the golden fiddle'*. She didn't know where it came from but she had always been tucked in between them, safe and warm, until everything went wrong.

She opened her eyes. It always came back to that. Even if this moment felt nice, it was this that was weird. Normal was the horrible stuff. Her eyes prickled with unexpected tears.

'I'm glad we're together on this,' she said, her voice thick. 'It's really bad here, isn't it?' She tucked her arms through theirs.

'Naylor is right about one thing at least,' Josh said. 'Look at the people. They're just going about their business, living under the volcano. Some of them have to know.'

Gabe cleared his throat. 'It's hard to face stuff sometimes.' He glanced at Kate.

She squeezed his arm. He had been through troubled times, at school and at home.

'Sometimes,' he went on, 'it's a hell of lot easier to just pretend that everything is alright. Watch.'

A couple were walking by. Kate recognised them vaguely. Gabe suddenly roared at them, making both Kate and Josh jump. The couple flinched but didn't look over or change their path.

'See, they don't care. No one wants to get involved. Just keep moving. If they don't look at us, they can pretend we don't exist.'

He settled against the back of the bench, sticking his feet out, his combat pockets chinking.

A white terrier appeared, sniffing around for scraps. Kate loved dogs and she let go of the boys' arms to lean towards it.

'Hey, little fella, c'mere!'

The dog paid her no attention. She called to it again but it didn't even look at her. It lifted its leg against a flowerpot and carried on, holding up one back leg every few steps.

'Dogs usually like me,' Kate said.

'It was like he didn't even see you,' Josh said.

Kate looked at him, then nudged Gabe.

'Gabe, do me a favour. Do that roar at the next people who walk by, will you?'

Gabe grinned and they waited. An old couple came by, but he shook his head.

'Don't want to give anyone a heart attack,' he said.

A gaggle of girls were coming their way, chatting and laughing, trying to show each other things on their phones despite the bright sunshine.

When the group were within touching distance of the bench, Gabe roared. The girls fell silent for one second, but didn't flinch. Instead, they restarted their chatter as if nothing had happened.

'That's not right,' Gabe said.

'You said that people pretend not to notice,' Josh said.

'Yeah, but I roared right at them. They should have screamed. I know those girls – they'd scream at anything.'

'I think we might be in trouble,' Kate said. 'Maybe this is not such a good idea. If something goes wrong out there, I don't think anyone will help us.'

'Let me go on my own then,' Josh said.

'No, we are all in this together. Kate's right,' Gabe said. 'Maybe you have those dreams and stuff, but there's a reason we're all involved. I say at least we go find out.'

Kate looked at him, surprised.

'Look, I don't talk about it much, but my dad drowned in a bloody well,' he said. 'It was a horrible way to go and now my mam only wants to knit and go to Mass and she's too young for giving up. What if we end up like that?'

'What if we end up losing wives and husbands too?' Josh added, going red.

'Look,' Gabe said. 'Just on the quay right now, I can see three, no, four people who've lost family to the river, not counting us. If Naylor is right, this has been going on for centuries. We have to do something. Because no one else will.'

'He's right, Kate,' Josh said, taking her hand. 'There has to be someone. I think there might always have been someone who tried and now it's our turn.'

'None of them succeeded. Or survived,' she said.

'No, but it's going to be different this time,' Gabe said.

Kate turned to him, offering her other hand. He took it and unselfconsciously kissed the back of it.

'Because it's us and we're different,' he said.

There was nothing more to say. They sat and held hands until the barge came back, then went up the gangplank, found seats on the deck close to the bow and went to war.

The barge went downstream under the bridge. Once they were well past the town, the river became quiet. It took a minute for Kate to realise that she felt better. Down this far, not only had they left the town behind, but they had crossed an invisible border into another county. A weight lifted off her chest and she was suddenly glad that her mother was away from Bailey. Surely, she must feel better. Kate looked at the boys. They were chatting about some Xbox game they both liked, as if there had never been any rivalry between them.

The other passengers were from outside town, most of them from overseas. The atmosphere was pleasant. Girls came up from the galley with an afternoon cream tea and they were greeted with a cheer. They laid out the tea, scones, cream and jam on a secured table in the stern of the boat and everyone helped themselves. Kate couldn't help herself. She smiled and chatted to the man next to her. He was telling her all about life in Texas when the barge slowed and began to turn.

The man seemed to forget what he was saying. He took a bite of his scone and wandered back to his wife. Kate looked around for Josh and Gabe.

Without a word, the three gathered together and went to their place near the bow.

The wispy clouds darkened and a few drops of rain fell. The girls quickly cleared the deck of food and everyone hurried below to the comfortable seats at the waterline.

Kate didn't move. Neither did the others. She tried to concentrate on her breathing, which had become shaky.

OK, it's happening. This is really happening.

The barge rounded a curve in the river and Bailey came into view.

Josh watched the town he had grown up in, as the mouse watches the owl.

'Look!' Kate cried.

Josh looked over the side to where she was pointing. Swimming half above the waterline, he saw the fur-covered backs of animals that might have been otters once. They swam with their noses over the water, sometimes dipping below the surface. They entwined with each other, breaching the surface, subsiding again, almost at play. Josh saw an ugly head rear up, the creature seeming to look up at him. He moved back from the rail and looked at Kate. Her face was white.

Gabe opened the pockets of his combat trousers and emptied them. He handed Josh and Kate a penknife each and advanced a blade on a Stanley knife for himself.

'Just in case this is about more than dreams,' he said, his teeth glinting.

Josh chuckled. If circumstances were different, maybe he could like Gabe after all.

Kate straightened her shoulders and looked grim. Josh exchanged a look with Gabe. It was a vow. They would do whatever was necessary to protect her. She was the centre of their group.

The water splashed at the rail. Josh caught a glimpse of black fur before it dropped back with a slap. He took a firm grip on the penknife and clicked out the blade. Kate did the same.

A beast, perhaps thrusting against its fellows, reared above the rail and fell inside the barge with a heavy thump. It sprang to its feet and hissed at them before turning its baleful glare on Josh. Its teeth were each as long as the penknife blade.

It lunged for him, but didn't get far. Gabe launched himself onto its thick back and sliced the Stanley knife across its neck, pulling the blade almost full circle. Blood gushed and the creature's head dropped to the deck, its body still writhing. Gabe was up fast but Josh had no time to see what he did next, because Kate screamed in what sounded more like rage than fear.

Another of the creatures had flung itself across the rail but its heavy body was pulling it back towards the

107

water. Kate thrust her knife at it, slashing its belly, drenching her arm in stinking ordure. She made a sobbing noise but shoved the creature backwards into the river. She was turning towards Josh when yet another made the attempt.

Bigger than the others, it reared above the rail, while still in the water. It jabbed its huge head at Kate and its jagged teeth caught the loose collar of her shirt. She screamed again, this time in terror, as she was dragged backwards. Josh threw himself forward, almost catching her. He was left with her sneaker in his hand as Kate disappeared over the rail into the water with the deadly monsters.

With no time for thought, Josh scrambled to his feet and dived over the rail. His dive brought him down through the mass of twirling bodies. He felt sharp teeth rip through his jeans, tearing his leg. He kicked hard and swam deeper before turning.

Something plunged into the water ahead. Gabe, turning awkwardly and kicking towards the black furred knot. Josh swam upwards and stabbed at dark flesh. The water turned red and Josh had to surface for a breath before diving down again. The barge had moved away.

This time, he saw a flash of white amid the black. A hand. He swam hard towards it, becoming aware of Gabe coming back from the surface to join him. They fought together, cutting, stabbing at the monsters. Josh saw the white hand again. He grasped it and pulled. He braced his feet against the knot of creatures and pulled harder. Kate shot out, barely recognisable in the bloody water, surrounded by chunks of furry flesh.

Josh kicked out at Gabe who was still slashing at the knot of creatures, hoping to signal that he had freed Kate and get him to leave the fray. He swam with one arm for the surface, pulling Kate behind him, but before he reached it he felt teeth sink into the flesh of his calf. He kicked, causing more pain. The creature shook him like a dog shakes a rat and he lost his grip on Kate.

He doubled over, stabbing with the knife at the beast that had him. It refused to let go and turned, dragging him to the bottom. His lungs were screaming and it was only a matter of time before they overrode his will and he took a breath that would be his last.

It was hard to see anything in the deep murk and the edges of his vision were darkening. He couldn't hold on any longer. He pleaded with anyone that might be listening that Kate would be OK. Then the world shut down on him.

'Then I will warn you to have a care, as you are now my enemy.'

Halley held out his hand. 'I won't give up on you, Nicholas.'

The abbot gripped his hand and they held still for a moment. In unspoken agreement to differ, they released each other and turned away.

Halley went down Sugar Lane to the quay and walked back with the familiar sounds of the docks in his ears. He knew what would come. As a boy, Nicholas Dunne had never given in. Even when he was held down and battered by other boys, he might cry and scream, but he would never give in. He wouldn't give in now either, but somehow Halley had to make him. He would have to talk to the others, but first he went to his own ship, now empty of the wine and spices he had brought. In a few days they would begin to load the fur and cloth that he was taking on his next voyage.

He climbed the gangplank onto the deck and went to the bow. William Marshall's oak bridge spanned a river that was bloody in the sunrise.

Halley stood there for a long time.

The noise of the docks was tremendous, but Halley still heard Barron's shout. The man's chest was like a barrel and years at sea had taught him to roar like the bear he resembled. Halley raised a hand and made his way down to the quay.

Barron met him, eyes blazing in the bearded face.

'Did ye meet?'

'Aye, we did.'

'Well?'

'He won't back down just on my word. Tell the others that we must go together tomorrow. We must show strength in numbers. If we all refuse, then he must back down. Tell the others to meet us at the tavern at dawn. We'll go to the abbey and talk some sense into the man.'

'Talk!' Barron exclaimed. 'This is not the time for talk, Halley!'

'We must start with talk and we have to be together on this. I know the man. We must be together.'

Barron started to protest again, but Halley laid a hand on his arm.

'Do it my way and let us see what happens.'

Barron's beard moved as he ground his jaw, but he nodded and slapped Halley on the back.

'Aye, we'll do it your way. Why else were we all waiting for you to come back? Now let's sup. There's plenty still to be had.'

Halley laughed and went towards the tavern with the big man. Tomorrow they would see what could be done.

He spent the day talking quietly to any of the captains who came his way. The serving girl came close to him and brought him food without him needing to ask for it. She often touched his shoulder as she went by. Halley watched the sway of her hips as his mind pondered other things.

He didn't say it to his friend, but Halley knew that talk wouldn't work. He had seen the truth of that in the abbot's eyes. By nightfall, he didn't feel fit to stay up drinking with the men. He went upstairs.

It was a long time before the girl finished her work and came up to him. He experienced the same rush of feeling in her arms, something akin to happiness. Afterwards, he lay down but his mind wouldn't rest. The girl slept, so deeply that he leaned close to see if she was breathing. Reassured of that at least, he stared at the beams, his thoughts running in circles. The light cast by the moon showed him a big spider making its way to the corner. He watched it until it disappeared and then he sat up. From the window, he could see the silver of the river in the moonlight.

He hoped to force the abbot to stop the toll by sheer numbers and weight of opinion. If they all stood together and refused to pay and told any others who came to port to refuse, then the friars couldn't enforce the toll. He still wanted to *prevent the violence he could see in the men's faces. He had swept aside arguments of going to the abbey tonight. He knew to go in darkness and anger was the way of the mob. He had seen enough of it on foreign shores. Daylight was the only way.*

But sleep wasn't going to come so Halley rose and dressed. He thought he would go to his ship. He longed for the feel of movement beneath his feet. Land only brought trouble. Being on the water was the beginning of freedom. He got out of bed and the girl stirred awake as he dressed.

'Stay there and sleep. I'll be back tomorrow,' he said.

She raised herself on her elbow and bit her lip. He smiled at her and shut the door quietly behind him.

He slipped down the back stairs and out through the scullery, walking through the filthy alleyway to the quay. He walked to the gates of the abbey, which stood open in welcome. He shut his eyes and said a silent prayer.

'Michael Halley, you're returned. Did I not warn you to have a care?'

He opened his eyes. The abbot was standing in front of him, a lantern set down at his feet, hands tucked into his habit to keep them warm from the chill of the night. The dwarf stood at the gate.

'You did, brother, but I came to warn you in turn. If you don't yield, there will be war.'

The abbot nodded. 'There will indeed, old friend. There will indeed.'

He tilted his head towards the dwarf, who darted forward. His gnarled hand came out from under his robe and the knife flashed .

The dwarf waved the knife casually in front of Halley, but his face was intent.

Halley didn't look at the knife but remained still, watching the dwarf's eyes. When he saw the change in his face that meant a lunge was coming, Halley reached out and grabbed his wrist. The dwarf's wrist was thick with heavy bones and sinews. He twisted and jerked out of Halley's grip. He lunged again and Halley caught his body, using one hand to hold the knife away from him. The dwarf rippled in his arms like a snake and the muscular torso flexed violently. Halley couldn't hold him. The knife went into Halley's side and he ground his teeth together against the scream that wanted to escape. The dwarf ripped the knife out and Halley felt like it had left some sizzling poison inside him. He shoved the dwarf as hard as he could and sent him flying backwards. He crashed to the ground on his back. The knife clattered out of his hand and Halley kicked it away. He kicked out again, this time connecting with the dwarf, feeling something crack under the impact. The dwarf cried out and turned onto his hands and knees. Halley kicked him again, sending him onto his belly this time. The dwarf cracked his head on the stones of the street and lay still. Halley's breath was coming hard and he felt the urge to help the man to his feet. He took a step forward when a tremendous weight hit him in the back. He stumbled forward and tried to take a giant step over the dwarf, but he tripped and fell at the abbot's feet. There was something on his back.

He tried to grab it but his fingers slipped on its greasy fur. He rolled over and heard it squeal as he crushed it. But it still gripped him. He struggled to his feet and tore at the thing. It sank its teeth into the back of his neck. He cried out and ran to

113

the abbey. He turned and launched himself backwards at the wall. He crushed the thing against the wall and ground it back and forth. A gush of liquid sprayed from the creature and he felt himself sink back into it. It squealed again and he felt it release its grip. He jumped away from it and looked back. It lay writhing on the ground. He couldn't identify it, but it had a thickly furred body and a dreadful face, almost childlike, but hideous.

'I can marshal forces that you don't even understand, Michael. Give up this fight now or lose everything.'

The abbot came in so close to Halley's face that he could smell the river on his breath. It smelt of death and stagnant water and other underlying things that Halley recognised but couldn't name.

The abbot's eyes were still blazing. 'I'll take everything you have. And everyone, including that serving wench that takes your fancy. I'll take her and rip her to shreds while she's still alive. I'll use her body for my pleasure and then tear her skin off. I'll do it over and over so she can suffer her death forever. Let me be or I'll do as I say.'

'You won't touch her. I'm going to stop you.'

Halley lunged at the abbot and wrapped his hands around his throat. The abbot brought his own hands up and gripped Halley's throat. They struggled together in silence until Halley started to feel himself blacking out. The other man was incredibly strong. His fingers felt like they were sinking into Halley's skin and his long nails were ripping his flesh. As his vision started to go, Halley let go of the abbot's throat and drove the heel of his hand into his nose. Blood spurted and a spot of it landed on Halley's cheek. It burned like hot oil. The

114

abbot let him go and Halley fell backwards, putting his hand on the abbey wall for support.

The abbot straightened up, blood streaming from his nose. He smiled at Halley and his teeth were red.

'So, we are evenly matched, as we always were,' the abbot said. 'Perhaps tomorrow we will finally be able to declare a champion.' He turned and walked away, leaving Halley staring after him.

Gabe grabbed Kate and made for the surface, adrenaline spurting through his bloodstream. He pushed himself onto the bank in one powerful movement and dragged her out of the water. He tried CPR and something akin to the Heimlich Manoeuvre until she finally started to cough up vomit and water. When she started to breathe properly and her lips were no longer blue, he flopped onto his back at her side.

'You seriously have to stop almost drowning,' he said.

'OK.' Her voice was hoarse but she was alive. 'Where's Josh?'

There was pain everywhere. Josh couldn't defend himself from further attacks. He was grabbed in rough hands and dragged. He felt like he was floating. Suddenly, there was light. He tried to take a breath but couldn't. A heavy fist thumped him in the middle of his back and water flew from his mouth. His face went under and he almost inhaled more, but he was dragged up by his hair. He couldn't see properly and gave

115

himself up to being first towed and then thrown onto hard ground. He lay there, just coughing and breathing until his head started to clear.

He opened his eyes and squinted against the light. He tried again and saw Kate and Gabe leaning over him.

'You're back. Good. Are you brain-damaged?' Gabe said.

'No more than you,' Josh managed.

'OK then.'

They helped each other to stand up. The towpath on this side of the bridge was little used, but they picked their way across it and made it back to Bailey. Even though they were all soaking wet and exhausted, no one looked at them, or spoke. They kept putting one foot in front of the other until they got to the cottage and collapsed – Josh onto an armchair, Kate and Gabe on the couch. They slept where they fell, passing the rest of the afternoon without stirring.

Chapter Seventeen

Halley was sick with anger and despair. He would have to lead the men against his old friend. He couldn't believe that such a change had been wrought in him in the year since he last traded in Bailey. But his mind whispered to him of stories, half heard and not believed, carried from seaman to seaman and reaching him in far-off places, tales of acts of violence and profligacy. He had dismissed them but he found himself remembering incidents from their childhood when Nicholas had proved to be ruthless. Even his taking to the life of a friar had been a ferocious decision, much against the wishes of his father and family. But once Nicholas had decided something, there was no dissuading him.

Keeping his hand pressed against his side where the dwarf's knife had cut him, he went wearily back to the Zephyros. His mind felt confused, going over and over everything. He needed to sleep. He would try his cabin.

Maybe the familiar bed would lull him into unconsciousness.

When he woke up, Josh lay still for a long moment, feeling an ache in his body. He ran his hands over his face and into his hair. He had dreamt again.

He sat up. Everything hurt.

Kate and Gabe were still tumbled together on the couch.

'You two look like I feel,' Josh said.

They stirred and gradually sat up, groaning.

'Was it worth it?' Kate asked, her voice hoarse.

'I'm not sure,' Josh said. 'I guess I found out some more stuff.'

'No. I mean ... *is* it worth it?'

Josh looked at her. She shook back her hair and met his gaze. For her, for Callum, for his parents, for himself, even for Gabe, it was worth it. Suddenly and with absolute certainty he knew he was doing what he was supposed to be doing.

'It's worth it,' he said.

Kate's eyelashes flickered but she didn't turn away from him. He wasn't able to help himself. He couldn't stop looking at her.

'Hey,' Gabe said. 'I'm OK, if anyone is interested. Remember me? The guy who saved both your lives?'

Kate hugged him and, just for a moment, everything felt alright.

Naylor was in the kitchen, scribbling in a notebook. Everyone sat down at the kitchen table in their usual places and Josh explained to Naylor what had happened on the river, and recounted his visions of the captain and the abbot.

'There's obviously a connection between you and this man you're dreaming of – or channelling,' Naylor said. 'We have to try the hypnosis again. I think you're very close to finding out what's going on,'

Josh was doubtful. He was reluctant to put himself in Naylor's hands.

'I'll see more when I sleep tonight. You don't need to hypnotise me.'

'But you didn't dream this afternoon.'

'I was too tired to dream.'

'Nevertheless, I'm not sure that you have the luxury of waiting,' Naylor said. 'Besides, you might subconsciously know something useful. I think it's important to try.'

'You're not afraid, are you?' Gabe said, pushing his chair back on two legs and smiling. Perhaps the ceasefire was over.

Josh narrowed his eyes. 'Fine. Do it then. But do it here. If I get too comfortable, I'll fall asleep properly before you can put me under.'

'Very well,' Naylor said.

He started talking quietly, his monotonous voice like the drone of insects in a sunny glade. Josh did find himself getting sleepy and he tried to hold Naylor's intense gaze without drifting off. He found himself thinking about the silence of his parents, a silence that was too big to break into.

A crash brought him out of his thoughts and he looked around. Gabe's chair legs had banged back to the floor and Gabe was sitting with his arms on the table, a distant look on his face.

'Gabe? What's the matter?' Kate asked.

'*Shh*,' Naylor said. 'He's under. I'll bring him out.'

'Wait,' Josh said. 'He's saying something.'

'*His plan won't work.*'

'Whose plan, Gabe?' Naylor asked.

'*That's not my name.*'

'Who are you then?'

'*Barron. My name's Charlie Barron. And Halley's plan won't work.*'

Barron sat up with some of his mates and warmed his big body with whiskey. Like the others, he looked up to Halley. The man was educated but more than that he was good. No one who knew him felt any differently about him. He drank with his men and had plenty of female company when he wanted it. He was tough and fought off pirates with extreme force when he needed to. He wasn't without flaws but he gave off something like a smell of goodness that most people found hard to resist. They would follow what he said.

But Barron knew that this time his plan wouldn't work. It couldn't work. The abbot wouldn't give in. It would take a show of strength, not will, to defeat him. Barron drank his whiskey and half listened to the men around him. He began to feel more and more that they were walking into trouble. He had to talk to Halley again. This time the man's judgement was blinded by his friendship with the abbot.

Barron stood up, his knees knocking against the table. The men cursed him but stopped when they saw his face. Barron went upstairs, but Halley wasn't there. A girl sat up in his bed, clutching the blanket to her chest, her chestnut hair falling on her shoulders, her green eyes wide.

Gabe shook himself all over like a dog and his eyes came back into focus. He stared at Kate and then lunged across the table at Josh. He grabbed his shirt and pulled him. They both staggered to their feet and Gabe pulled back his arm to throw a punch.

'*Gabe!*'

Kate's voice made him pause and he frowned and shook his head.

Josh struck his hand away and came around the corner of the table.

'*Stop it, both of you!*' Kate's voice was furious.

Gabe straightened up. He looked at her face and put his hands on her arms. He pulled her close to him and kissed her hard on the lips. She wrenched herself away. Josh put his hand on Gabe's shoulder and shoved him backwards. Gabe grabbed at a chair and almost fell with it, then straightened and took a step forward.

Kate put herself between him and Josh.

'*Stop it! Gabe, what are you doing?*'

'Katie. Is there something going on between you two?' Gabe said.

Josh stepped around Kate. 'What about it if there is?'

'Josh, shush, please,' Kate said. 'Gabe, nothing is going on. We're all in this together.'

'Kate, you don't know how I feel.'

'I do, Gabe. I'm just not ready for anything. With anyone.'

Gabe looked at Josh and saw a flicker in his eyes. It was true. At least there was still a chance if she hadn't started up with him. He looked at Josh over her head. Josh nodded slightly. When this was over, they would see.

All three of them had forgotten Naylor who had sat silent through all this, studying the dynamics of the little group intently.

Chapter Eighteen

For once, Kate was glad when everyone was gone. She had gone from being desperately lonely to being part of a circle. It was important and she was glad of their company and help. They had somehow come together and formed a unit. They needed each other. But still, she sometimes felt like the air was full of jealousy and competition. She could see that both Josh and Gabe were looking at her and glaring at each other. Doc Naylor kept looking at Josh in an odd way. She didn't trust Naylor and she felt a funny rush of bitterness that she didn't recognise at first. Josh was handsome and sort of fascinating to look at, and maybe Naylor saw that too.

Josh felt very different to hug than Gabe. Gabe was big and hard and muscular and he was good to hug. He had big strong arms to wrap her up. When she felt vulnerable, that was nice. She just didn't like feeling vulnerable.

Josh was leaner and younger-looking and different. Josh made her nervous. Hugging him made her feel fizzy and odd and adult.

She suddenly realised what the bitter feeling was. She was jealous. Jealous because horrible old Naylor was looking at Josh. She felt some guilt, because Naylor was trying to help them. Then her common sense kicked in. Last year, she might not have known the difference, but a lot had happened since then. She had grown up a bit. She hadn't had a choice. Naylor looked at Josh in a particular way, but Josh seemed neither to notice or care. Besides, he and Gabe were too busy trying to outdo each other.

Sometimes she just wanted both of them to stop and give her a minute. Even the house smelt different with them in it.

She wanted to read. She wanted a bath. Mostly she wanted a rest from everyone. She picked up a book she hadn't finished and ran the taps. Once she got into the bath, she lost interest in the book and just lay in the warm water, gazing at the wall. It felt good to do nothing. She closed her eyes and knew she was close to sleep. She moved her feet to keep herself from drifting off. The sound of the water lapping against the side of the bath was pleasant.

After a while, she became sleepier and it seemed harder to move her feet. The water felt viscous. She opened her eyes and found herself lying in a bath of blood. A great fat drop of blood dripped from the tap and made ripples in the surface. She lunged up, splashing blood in her face, and fell out onto the floor.

She struggled to her feet, slipping in gore. As she reached the door, she heard the blood in the bath slop onto the floor and she slammed the bathroom door without looking back.

It crept under the door, making her back away, but it became more viscous and stopped moving after a couple of inches. Kate could smell it on herself. She hurried to the other bathroom, trying not to slip, leaving bloody footprints. She let the water in the shower run for five minutes before carefully getting in, constantly watching the stream in case it changed. The worst moments were when she washed her hair with a shower gel. With her eyes closed, she was convinced the blood was streaming over her again.

Opening her eyes, she screamed, so sure was she that there would be blood again. She laughed shakily when she saw clean soapy water running into the drain, but didn't waste any time rinsing herself off and getting out. Wrapping herself in a towel, she fetched a mop from under the stairs and retraced her steps, wiping up as she went.

At the main bathroom door, she hesitated, then opened it quickly with a hard push. It made a sucking noise as it pulled free of the sticky blood under it. Nothing was dripping from the tap, neither blood nor water.

She wasn't about to tackle the room wrapped in just a towel, so she went and dressed in old clothes and boots before starting.

The smell was the worst. Metallic and gross. She began to recite poems to herself in an effort to distract from the task. By the time she finally finished, she realised she was saying the prayers of her childhood. *As I lay me down to sleep ...*

She stood in the middle of the bathroom with fury rising in her. She knew she had friends but she wasn't supposed to be alone here at home. She was supposed to still have her parents. She wasn't supposed to be mopping up blood when she should have been going shopping, or hanging out. She threw the mop into the bath and ran downstairs and outside.

She went to the edge of the river and screamed, at first without words, but then words came.

'You killed my father and took my mother from me! All I wanted was to have a bloody bath!'

She fell silent and shocked herself by laughing. A bloody bath was what she'd had alright. She laughed at whatever might have been listening and then threw a rock into the water, before going back inside. Her laughter almost turned to tears and she recognised that she was being hysterical. She put the mop away, changed her clothes and put the kettle on.

By the time she sat down with tea, the tears had come and gone. She left most of the tea in the mug, a wave of exhaustion sweeping over her. She went slowly to bed, with no idea if anything would happen in the night. Tired as she was, she expected to lie awake, waiting.

Despite herself, her eyes closed. and she saw Josh's face. Square jaw, gorgeous blue eyes, untidy hair, something indefinable that drew her which had nothing to do with his looks. Despite herself, she pictured him kissing her and knew that was what she wanted. But not yet. How could she even think of going out with someone with everything that was going on? What would they do? Go to the cinema? Ridiculous. She didn't know if any of them would survive this. Plus there was Gabe to consider. She knew he wanted to be with her and anything else would break his heart. Did she have to break someone's heart just to be happy herself?

She didn't even want to be happy anyway, she just wanted to be normal and have some fun. Happy was a distant emotion to do with long-term relationships. It would just be nice if she could have a few dates and kiss the boy she liked but it seemed too much to ask on top of surviving.

She was proud that she had managed since her mother went to hospital; proud of the money she had started to earn with her paintings. She wanted friends to help her fight whatever was plaguing her home town. She also wanted to be independent and strong and to belong to herself.

But she was too honest to ignore it. She wanted to be with Josh. She groaned and turned over, trying to find the elusive spot that would allow her to sleep. Then she heard a voice calling her. Someone or something outside in the river, calling to her, laughing back at her. A voice filled with mud. She pulled the cover over her head and tried to ignore it.

Halley wasn't like the others. He wasn't rough or demanding. He was gentle with her. He looked at her like she mattered.

127

Maybe it was only for a few hours at a time but, when he looked at her like that, she felt like she could be free.

Her uncle owned the inn and she had worked here since her mother had gone to the leper colony. She knew she was lucky not to catch the leprosy but she still wished for her mother. In the beginning she had crept close to the village where her mother lived with the others, but she was spotted and they threw stones at her and led her mother away, crying. It was only to keep her safe, but it was horrible just the same. She stopped going. It made her too sad.

Her uncle was a hard man, not cruel, but not nice either. He fed her and made her work, and beat her if she needed it. She had seen Halley before but he hadn't noticed her. This time when she'd heard he was coming back, she had sewn two dresses together to make a good one, like new. She washed herself until her skin was red and arranged her hair carefully, tying it up with a ribbon that someone had left behind, jealously guarded from the other girls.

She smiled brightly at him when he came in and served him quickly. He smiled back at her and seemed to see her this time. He was not the only kind man she had ever seen. His friend Barron was kind too, but Halley was the only man who was gentle and kind to everyone. She knew that everyone thought well of him. He was her only chance for a life without cruelty.

She didn't know then that she would love him. They had been together twice now and she knew. She thought he felt something too. It was in his eyes when he held her close. He seemed to study her before he kissed her and, although his kisses were passionate, they were also sweet.

128

He left the bedroom to attend to some business and she lay there, dreaming of him and of the life they might have together. He would take her on board his ship and they would cross the seas. Although it was night, she thought she heard the seagulls and the slap of the water against the ship's wooden flanks.

They would marry on some foreign shore and she would never again serve any man food or ale but him. They would lie together every night and there would be children. She put her hand on her belly. Maybe a child had already started. Halley would look wonderful holding their child. He was tall and lean and his handsome face was kind. She knew that they would have an eternity together.

The door banged open and Barron ducked under the frame.

'Where is he?'

'He went out. I don't know where.'

Barron stood in silence for a moment.

'I do,' he said and thumped down the narrow stairs.

She stared after him, fear running through her veins. She threw back the rough sheet and pulled on her dress and shoes. She ran downstairs and outside. She saw his broad back crossing the quay and followed him. He was heading for the Zephyros.

Chapter Nineteen

Richard went back into the surgery, having finished his house call. He sat down at his desk but didn't buzz for the next patient. He picked up the silver pen that Lynn had given him as part of a set for his last birthday. He began to doodle lines on his blotter. He leaned heavier and heavier on it, making deep marks. He lifted the pen and stabbed it down at the blotter, then pulled it along, scoring deep wounds in the surface.

That heavy girl. Who was she? She meant something but he didn't want to think about what. He shook his head, trying to shake the headache free. He had never suffered from migraines before but lately he understood the desire to bash his head against the wall to alleviate the pain. He put the pen nib to his hand in the loose skin between thumb and index finger. He pressed it as hard as he could into his skin and grunted with the effort.

The pain took the headache away and he dropped the pen. A tear rolled from his eye and landed on the edge of the blotter. It magnified a red letter advertising the drug company that had given him the blotter. The colour made the teardrop fat and bloody. He rubbed his fingers under his eyes, pushing his glasses askew as he did. He settled them back on his nose and pressed the buzzer for the next patient.

Alma came out of the woods. She walked up to the house and went around the back. The door was open. She went into a small utility room and then into an open-plan kitchen/living room. It was lovely, all bright and full of eclectic furniture. She stood with her hand on the kitchen table.

Kate walked into the kitchen. She stared.

'Alma? What are you doing here?'

Alma walked around the corner of the table. Her head was buzzing and it was hard to keep the smile on. Kate took a step back. Alma kept walking.

Kate turned and ran, but Alma grabbed her long hair as it flew out behind her. She jerked her arm back. Kate screamed and fell back into Alma's arms. She weighed nothing. Alma dragged her along the kitchen, with an arm around her neck. Kate was struggling and scratching. Alma tightened her grip around her neck and she started to make choking noises. She didn't give up though. She was trying to wrap her legs around the table legs. Alma gave her one huge pull and flung her sideways. She forced her into the utility room and threw her to the floor. She pulled at the back door, intending to get the girl to the river.

She turned, almost in time, before a tremendous weight struck her head. She went down onto her hands and knees and felt a moment of confusion. What was she doing in this utility room on the floor? The buzzing made it hard to think. A sudden image of the boy filled her mind. She wanted him so much. She started unsteadily to get up but, before she had regained her balance, Kate ran at her and toppled her through the back door, slamming it behind her.

Alma turned and pounded at the locked door. The pain started to clear from her head. She banged at the door for another few minutes, then frowned. She couldn't quite remember why she was there. She backed away from the door, suddenly afraid that someone would answer. She didn't want to talk to anyone.

Hurrying, she went back to the public pathway, all the time conscious that someone from the house might call after her. Once she rounded the bend in the towpath, she felt better. Slowing down, she trudged towards home, not quite sure what had happened. She was just out for her walk, but she'd got another headache. She was getting lots of them lately. She had better go to see that doctor. That nice new doctor.

Chapter Twenty

There was a knock at his bedroom door and Josh got up to answer it. Kate had been so much on his mind that he thought for a second that he had conjured her up. His mother must have let her in.

Kate stood there, staring at him, unsmiling. She was wearing some sort of old-fashioned dress.

'Kate. What's the matter? Did something happen?'

She put her hand on his chest and even though he could feel how cold her hand was, her touch seemed to burn into his skin through his T-shirt. She pushed him and he stepped back to let her into the room. He shut the door and turned to her. She folded herself against him and kissed his throat. He put his arms around her and bent to kiss her. When she kissed him back, he felt like he couldn't breathe. He tangled his hands in her hair and she combed her fingers into his. She moved back, still kissing him. He followed, lost in her. When she reached the bed, she sank back, pulling him with her. She was so serious, expressionless almost, except for her eyes which seemed to burn.

She raised her arms over her head and lay there watching him. Her skin was so creamy. He drank her in. He felt as if he could never get enough of just looking at her. But somehow he was allowed to touch her.

He leaned in to kiss her again. She tasted like fresh water. He shook his head. He couldn't believe this was happening. He looked into her lovely face and saw something there that made him falter. Some curious doubling of his vision. She smiled at him but he didn't move. She tried to pull him down to her.

'Kate, stop. I ...'

She pulled him harder and buried her face in his neck. He could smell her. It was a smell of damp and moss. As soon as he realised it, the smell intensified and he gagged. Her face twisted and he saw something hiding behind her skin. He tried to pull away but she clung to him, grabbing with her hands and clamping him with her thighs. Her face changed and he saw her features become muddy and wet. He yelled and struggled but her hands became claws and bit into him. Her body changed and sank away from him. Her face was dark and clogged with dirt now, but it morphed into the face of the dwarf of his dreams.

'Get out!' it snarled. 'Get out or you'll be dead, the same as everyone else! *Get out, get out, getoutgetoutgetout!*'

Josh struck at it. His fist sank into its muddy face

134

and it became formless and fell back onto the bed, splashing against him in a wave of foul-smelling muck. He cried out and leapt from the bed. There was nothing left but mud.

The image of Kate beneath him flashed through his mind and he turned away from the bed.

It wasn't her. Don't think about it. It wasn't her.

He showered, threw the dirty bedclothes in the washing machine and set it going.

He found his parents in the sitting room, watching morning TV with the curtains closed. He explained to them that he thought it would be better if they got out of town for a while, maybe go to Dublin to his aunt. He expected resistance but got none. Instead, with an air of relief, they threw things into bags, called Josh's aunt and were ready to go within the hour. His mother tried once to convince him to go with them, but it was easy to assure her that he'd be fine. He ushered them into the car and waved them off. He was glad to see that his dad seemed focused on driving. The main thing was that they were out of Bailey and safe.

As soon as they were out of sight, he set off, walking fast. He needed to see Kate. He hesitated where the road split. He should take the road and not the towpath. The river was dangerous but he was through running away from things. Callum would have taken the towpath. If he had to run through danger, then so be it.

When he reached the cottage, he was almost disappointed that nothing had happened. He felt fired up and ready to fight. The back door was closed and everything had an air of being too quiet. Something was wrong. He rapped on the door with his knuckles and waited. No one came. He went around to the kitchen window and knocked on that. He heard Kate's voice inside calling his name, then heard the back door being unlocked. He hurried back around and Kate grabbed his arm and pulled him in, slamming the door behind him and locking it. When she turned to face him, she was trying not to cry and she buried her face in his chest. He put his arms around her.

After a shuddering moment, she turned her head to look at him and smiled shakily. Her face was white.

'Kate. What happened?' He looked at her throat and saw the mark of bruising starting to come up.

'Alma came into the house. She grabbed me.'

'Who?'

'Alma Fitzgerald. She's a year ahead in school. She's a big girl, always in dark clothes?'

Josh nodded. He had seen her around.

Kate's voice was hoarse. 'Anyway, she put her arm around my neck and pulled me through the kitchen. She was trying to get me out of the house. She was much stronger than me. She would have got me out or in the river or I don't know what but I picked up the copper pan.' She grimaced. '*Ugh*, I hit her with it. It was gross, but it knocked her down and I got her out somehow. She just went away.'

He held her close to him again. He wanted to kiss her so badly. He wanted to make everything right for her. The sight of injury on Kate's skin made him burn inside. She squeezed him back. He felt a heavy weight on his chest making it hard to breath. He took a deep hitching breath.

She patted his back and moved away, her hair hiding her face. He went to the window and looked out at the river.

'Something happened at home. You came to me, Kate. At least, something that looked like you. But it was made of … I don't know, the river or something out of it.'

'That's horrible.'

He turned around. 'I want to go to the place where the abbey used to be.'

'We've been through this before. You're not going on your own,' Kate said.

'I'm not risking anyone coming with me.'

'This is not just your problem. You can't take it all on yourself.'

Josh frowned. He wanted to protect her but he didn't know if he could take being so close to Kate all the time without being able to kiss her at least. But he still didn't really know what was going on with her and Gabe and she had a kind of wall around her that stopped him getting close. But the apparition had shown him that he did want more than to be her friend. They needed to talk about stuff, but right now he just wanted to have her beside him. So he nodded.

'We'll go together.'

'When?'

'Tonight? Tomorrow morning? Whatever makes it worse, I want that. I want to confront it. I feel like it's the

137

only way to do this.'

'Let's try in the morning then. Early. Sometimes, things feel funny before the dawn, different, closer to the past or something?' She was intense and determined. 'We should go before the sun rises properly.'

'We have to think of a way to protect you then,' Josh said. 'Us, I mean,' he amended when she glared at him. 'What about the internet first for ideas, call Doc for the location of the abbey, eat dinner and confront evil for dessert?'

Kate smiled and he felt better. He froze the picture in his mind. He was going to save every image of her, every word she spoke. He smiled back and squeezed her arm.

Chapter Twenty-one

Richard buzzed for his last patient. He jotted some notes while waiting. The door opened and closed. He put aside his notebook before looking up.

The large girl from the quay was standing just inside the door, smiling at him.

'Hello, doctor.'

'Hello.'

Richard felt pain drilling into his temples. The pain ate away at his focus. He looked up at her again. She had moved closer. She sat down and rested her elbows on his desk. He stared in fascination at the wedge of fat in the bend of her arm.

'You know what I'm here for.'

Richard shook his head, frowning. He opened his mouth to snarl the word no. He felt his lips sneer back from his teeth but a gigantic burst of pain pounded behind his eyes and he almost slumped on the desk. He felt like crying but he said yes.

'What are we going to do?' she said.

Richard felt his hand reach out. He looked at it as if it belonged to another person. He took her hand and stroked his thumb across her dry skin the way he would with his wife.

'We're going to take care of it.'

'He'll be mine?'

'For a little while. Before the end.'

She laughed then, a delighted little-girl laugh. Richard took his hand back. A tear blurred his eye and when he blinked it made a prism on his eyelashes.

Chapter Twenty-two

Josh hung up the phone. Doc had been talking to him about the history of the abbey.

'It belonged to an order called the Brothers of the Cross,' he told Kate. 'They were there in the thirteenth century. Apparently they tended to the sick. There was a leper colony outside the town wall back then.'

'Leprosy? Here in Bailey?'

'Yes. It was quite common in those times, he said.' He paused. 'OK. I've been thinking about these dreams or whatever. Halley went to see the abbot at dawn, so I think it's right to go then. Maybe the abbot will put in an appearance.'

'That feels right,' Kate agreed.

'But, and I know you're going to argue and we agreed to go together ...' Josh paused. 'Halley went alone to the abbot and I think I should too. I think the dreams have to serve a purpose, Kate. It's not only that I want to keep you safe, but I think it's the way it's meant to be done. I don't think any of this stuff is coincidence, do you?'

Kate looked worried but shook her head.

'I suppose not.'

'Will you stay then and let me do it alone?'

'No.'

'Kate.' He stopped. 'Will you at least wait for me in the street and not come right in if we find the abbey? I honestly think I'll have a better chance of getting close to him by myself.'

She furrowed her brow. 'That does make sense but I just don't like it. I feel like we should stick together.'

'I know. I have to ask you to trust me. I really think I have to do this.'

'I ... do trust you.'

Josh let out a breath. As long as she was safe.

The evening passed quickly. Josh found himself wishing it could last forever. They laughed a lot and kept the TV loud to drown out any noises from outside or fears from inside. There were several moments where he thought he might lean in for a kiss, but each time she felt it too and moved or changed the subject.

Josh slept on the couch, with his feet hanging over the edge. He heard some noises in the night and, somewhere around three o'clock, he heard Kate's bed creak as she turned over. He turned over awkwardly on the sofa and pictured her tucked into his arms, imagining her back pressed against him. It took him a long time to drift off again.

He woke up in the grey pre-dawn light and sat up. He was stiff and the cottage was early-morning chilly. He had slept in his clothes, so he just pulled on his sneakers and washed his face at the kitchen sink. He ran his wet hands through his hair and felt the stubble on his chin.

He was about to slip out of the house when she came downstairs, wearing a woolly jumper with lots of darns in it.

She didn't speak but put her arms around him. He hugged her back. He buried his face in her hair and kissed her cheek, moving slowly towards her mouth. He kissed her softly and she held him tight for a second but then slipped out of his arms. It was hard to let her go, but time was moving on.

Without speaking, they left the house and stepped into a morning that felt out of place.

Josh wanted to be in Abbey Street before dawn really came. The path was wreathed in thin mist which wound around their ankles and made the path seem like some unknown trail. The birds had been singing around Kate's house, but out here next to the river everything was quiet. The river itself was blanketed in thick fog. It was eerie, but he didn't think anything would try to stop him getting to the abbey. He felt he was meant to go there. He just didn't know if that was a good thing or a bad one.

They went along Abbey Street and when Josh took Kate's hand she didn't pull away.

Josh stopped at the spot where Doc had said the abbey once existed. There was a row of houses there now. They walked down along them until they came to a small gate that closed a tiny alleyway between that row and the

143

next. Josh leaned over the gate and opened it. The alley was scruffy and overgrown with weeds. Someone had thrown a beer bottle over the gate.

'OK,' he said quietly. 'I'm going in through here. I feel this is it. Wait for me?'

She nodded and took his hand again, squeezing it. Her fingers were cold. Josh thought about kissing her again, but he hesitated and the moment was lost.

He went through the gate and the alley opened into communal gardens. Some of the occupants had put up some fencing, but there was a great open space in the centre that was untended. Josh would have expected to see evidence of this being a hook-up spot or a drinking spot or both, but it was clean. There were no cigarette butts or broken glass, no garbage of any kind. The grass and weeds were long, but the area looked deserted rather than badly used.

He went to the centre of the space, stepping around growths of stinging nettles and brambles. The backs of the houses looked blank. There were few windows in the backs and all their curtains were pulled. He was reminded of Robert Louis Stevenson's description of Mr. Hyde's residence with its *'blind forehead of discoloured wall'* and *'marks of prolonged and sordid negligence'* in *Dr. Jekyll and Mr. Hyde.*

He looked at the few tendrils of fog that had drifted in here from the river. Some pink was creeping into the sky. He closed his eyes and thought about his dreams, trying to recapture the feeling of them.

The dwarf pulled the dark cloak around him. It pooled around his feet and covered his head. He shrank into the meagre shadow cast by a huge coil of rope. The captain turned away. His back was vulnerable, but the time wasn't right. After a while, he turned and went below. The dwarf heard the creaking of the ship as he went into his quarters. When the movement stopped, he shed the robe and crept towards the hatch and went down. He had explored earlier and knew where to go. The way was dark but shot through with thin beams of light from the moon. He paused outside the door of the captain's cabin and waited. He listened while the captain moved on the bed and he gave him time to settle into sleep. The dwarf's body was in pain, standing still for so long, but he had endured worse. When he heard a light snore, he opened the door.

He moved forward, shuffling. When he reached the bedside, he studied the captain. His handsome face and long straight body looked to be bound by sleep. The dwarf withdrew the knife from its sheath, the blade flashing in the moonlight. He moved closer and, reaching over the bed, held the knife to the exposed throat. Then before the captain could stir, he buried the knife in the side of his neck and pulled it towards him, slicing the flesh open.

The captain screamed, his voice gurgling as the dark blood flooded from his flesh. He jerked half up before flopping back, his hands clutching at his throat. The blood spurted and spilled, looking black in the moonlight.

The dwarf stood back out of reach as the captain's body convulsed. He saw his eyes and knew that he understood what was happening. He knew what the captain saw: the deformed body and misshapen head, the blood-covered knife, the familiar face. He was the last person the dying man would ever see. Pip

Long, always known as Long Pip. And the captain knew whose hand had commanded his knife.

'Josh, are you alright?'

Josh squinted his burning eyes. Naylor was looking at him, his face concerned.

'I know what happened to Halley. The abbot had him killed. His servant – the dwarf – did it. Cut his throat. '

'Did you … feel it?'

Josh nodded. 'It was Halley, but it was me as well.'

'Then perhaps we won't learn any more from his perspective,' Naylor said.

'I guess not. But what are you doing here?' Josh looked around. 'Where is Kate?'

'Kate? I haven't seen her.'

'I left her outside … beyond the alleyway.'

'No sign of her,' Naylor said.

Josh shivered. Dawn was over and the day had begun.

Chapter Twenty-three

Kate hadn't liked it when he went off by himself. They should stay together. Sometimes, it was hard to believe that anything could be wrong. The morning smelt great, with a feeling of coming sunshine, all fresh and warm. A seagull cried harshly over the river. Kate walked slowly down the path towards the quay and looked upriver. There was a small boat coming out from under the bridge. A young man waved at her, saying something she couldn't hear. When he was close to the quay, he threw a rope to Kate, who caught it and tied it to a cleat on the dock.

'Hi, isn't it a beautiful day?'

He seemed so happy that Kate smiled at him. He had a black Labrador who was waving his thick tail at her.

'What's your dog's name?'

'That's Benny. He's a good boy, aren't you, Benny?'

Benny's mouth fell open in a doggy laugh.

'How far are you going?' Kate said.

'As far as the river goes, we're following,' he said. 'Why don't you come with us, Kate?'

Kate looked at him. His eyes were blue, like Josh's. She felt a bit woozy when she looked into them. He smiled at her and he looked like Josh then too. She dragged her gaze away, feeling like her neck was too weak to hold her head up properly.

'Come on, Kate, let's go for a spin. It'll be fun. I'll look after you.'

Kate smiled. He was right, it would be fun. It was a shame to live next to the water and never get to do anything on it. She stepped closer to the edge. He took her hand and helped her into the boat.

'Don't be afraid, Kate. It'll be fun,' he repeated.

Kate looked at the dog. His doggy face had looked like he was laughing before, but now it looked like he was snarling at her. His eyes were red and saliva trailed from his open mouth in a sticky trail.

'Josh,' she said, the word sounding sludgy in her mouth. She swallowed. 'Josh, I think the dog is thirsty.'

'Don't worry about the dog, Kate. Little Kate.' Josh's voice sounded funny too.

Kate looked at him. There was something wrong with his face. It looked muddy. His fingers were starting to bite into Kate's arm.

'Josh, you're hurting me. Not so tight.'

Josh's head rolled forward, almost knocking into Kate's face. Kate tried to say something else but her mouth wouldn't form the words. She felt all wrapped up and it was hard to breathe. He grinned at her and Kate saw something move in his eyes. She looked away and watched the water flowing by. The river was brown but, up close like this, Kate could see things moving under the surface. She could see streams of green weeds flowing and little fish darting in and out.

She stared in wonder as a great black salmon began to keep pace with the boat. It swam with a languorous movement that reminded her of a shark. It looked black enough to be sucking all the light into itself. She found it hard to keep her chin from dropping onto her chest, but she couldn't take her eyes off the salmon. It turned to look at her and its face seemed human almost. Kate grimaced but felt her face react slowly, feeling stiff, as though she had been to the dentist.

The salmon dived and she couldn't see it anymore. But the water was lovely. She let her body lean forward until she was lying over the edge of the boat with her hands trailing in the water. It was so cool. The breeze of the boat's movement was so pleasant on her stiff face. She couldn't think what was wrong when everything felt so nice. Her ponytail fell over her shoulder and the tip of it touched the water. She lowered her head a bit more and then her hair looked like the green stuff flowing under the surface. She could smell the cool scent of the water and felt an urge to put her face into it. Her cheeks felt so hot. She leaned over a little more and felt Josh's hand on her back. He would keep her safe.

The water touched her face and she gasped. Josh's

hand stroked her back and she relaxed. She opened her mouth and let the water play against her lips. The boat wasn't going fast enough for the water to hurt her. Anyway, the water wouldn't hurt her. She leaned a bit more and felt herself begin to slide. Her eyes drifted closed. Everything was fine. She just felt so tired. The water would be lovely. It would hold her up and everything could just drift. She started to slip into the river. There was something in there. She clung to the side of the boat and squinted. The object moved and she saw her father's face.

She jerked back and looked at the man in the boat with her.

It wasn't Josh.

She threw herself back onto the seat and looked for something to defend herself with. The man lunged at her, his face contorted. She scratched his face, aiming for his eyes, but he was oblivious. She fought hard but she was no match for his strength. With the boat rocking violently, he picked her up and threw her at the water.

She went deep under and fought for the surface. She broke through and gasped air. The water was cold and greasy this close to town. Something bumped against her and Kate looked around wildly. There was nothing floating beside her but the bridge was ahead. She didn't want to go under the bridge. It was dark in there.

She kicked around in a circle, looking for the boat. It was gone and there was no one else on the river. After the bridge, downstream, there were a few villages but the river was very wide until it got to the sea. Kate started to kick for the shore. But the river had her, sweeping her under the bridge. She scrabbled at the piling close to her, trying to find purchase. Finally, her fingers found a groove in the concrete and she hung on.

She was still in darkness but she wasn't being swept downstream. She hung on for a while, catching her breath and trying not to panic. She couldn't remember how she had got in the river. She looked up at the darkness above her and shrieked when something moved up there. A pigeon dropped from the darkness and flew out from under the bridge in a flurry of wings. Kate drew a deep breath. It smelt bad under here.

Her arms were getting tired. She inched her fingers higher in the crack, afraid to let go. She couldn't stay here forever and she didn't think anyone was coming to rescue her so she took a deep breath and kicked away from the piling. She swam towards the next piling, feeling strain in her neck as she tried to keep her head above water. She swam at an angle to it, so that when she stopped the outgoing tide kept her against the bottom of the piling. She stretched her arms up and hung onto the concrete, catching her breath. She would use the pilings to cross the river to where the river bank sloped gradually into the water. She didn't think she could pull herself up onto the dock on the town side. The tide was getting too low.

Chapter Twenty-four

Adam checked out his reflection as he walked down Abbey Street. The sun was shining and he was looking and feeling good. Days had passed since he had left the redhead in the old house and nobody had come to him yet. A few people had seen them leave the club together but she wasn't even being mentioned on the news anymore. His mother had driven by the old house out of curiosity and there was police tape around the door but no cops or cars or anything.

So Adam figured he was off the hook. The girl probably just had a heart attack from the ecstasy anyway. It wasn't his fault. That thing he saw was just him freaking out after a bad tablet or something.

Anyway, it was fine now. Nothing had happened and it was getting close to the weekend. There was a blonde he was going after on Saturday. She had been giving him the eye.

A woman passed by, glancing at him. He put his tongue out at her and wagged it. She winced and turned away. Adam laughed and walked on.

He was meeting Jerry and the lads at the end of the old bridge to have a few drinks. They were already on the benches when he got there.

'Hey, Jerry. Give us a beer.'

Jerry looked up at him.

'There's only one each.'

Adam swore and took a can. The metal was sweating and cold. He popped it and drank deeply. He gathered himself and belched, trying to form words as he did. He sat down on a bench, finished the can and threw it into a flower barrel.

'What am I going to drink now then, you useless tosser?'

Jerry was the only one of them working and he was always complaining that he had to buy everything. His mother was loaded though and doted on her only child, so he usually came up with the goods.

Mark was sitting on the ground with his back to the railings.

'I've got something. Frank brought it back from Chad.' Mark's brother was in the army and his visits home were often a lucky dip of cool stuff he picked up abroad.

'Why didn't you say so? What is it?'

Mark said nothing as some old fella walked by.

Adam clicked his fingers. 'C'mon. Give it here.'

Mark got up. He dragged a bit of tinfoil from his jeans

153

pocket and came over. He opened it and showed them. The things in the foil looked like cod-liver-oil capsules.

'What are they?' Adam said.

'Don't know. He said it's like acid.'

'It'll get me high, right?'

'Yeah.'

Adam took one of the capsules and swallowed it. The others followed suit. He sat back on the bench and waited to see what would happen.

The woman walked briskly towards the old bridge. She patted her hair. She loved that just-out-of-the-salon feeling. She never washed her own hair – she always had it done professionally. She had her nails freshly done at the same time. She caught sight of herself in a window. She was fifty next year but felt she looked only about thirty-five.

As she approached the bridge she saw some young men lounging around there. She felt a little anxiety about passing them, but it was a lovely morning during the week. Nothing would happen. When she came closer, the sound of her heels made them look up. There was something wrong with their eyes and the way they stared at her made her skin prickle. They looked like … like wolves. A sort of scent came off them that made her gasp. She stopped and stared at them.

They stood and fell into a formation like a pack. The one at the front licked his lips. He took a step forward and wavered slightly. Then he straightened himself and came up to her. He put his face close to hers and she could smell his breath. It smelt of some sweetness that she couldn't place. He pulled her hair and made her look at him, then put out his tongue and licked her lips. She was both disgusted and excited.

There were cars passing and people in the street. She was aware of being watched but she couldn't move away. He leaned in again and kissed her roughly. She kissed him back and he bit her lip. She tasted her own blood. He swayed backwards and smiled at her, his teeth red with her blood. She could hear the others breathing, panting almost. He fell on her then and the others snarled and crowded around him, on their knees.

Josh strode around the apartment. The window had been fixed but was standing open, letting a nice breeze in.

Naylor was wearing shorts and had his skinny legs crossed. His feet were in sandals and his bony toes protruded. He hadn't shaved yet and his angular jaw was bristly.

'How come you found me anyway?' Josh asked.

'I had an odd idea this morning. It got me up early. Just had a funny feeling I should go out and take a look at the day. I heard something. It might be more accurate to say I felt something. I reached the gate at the mouth of the alley and stopped there. And somehow I felt compelled to go inside. I went through and looked around. It was misty in there and as I watched a form started to appear in the mist and got more solid and there you were, bloody and bruised.'

'Thanks for the shirt. Again.'

Naylor waved his hand. 'How is the wound now?

Josh pulled up the loose shirt. He had washed all the blood off and all that was left on his side was a thin scar that looked like it had been there for years.

Naylor leaned forward and touched the mark.

'Fascinating.'

He sat back and Josh dropped the shirt, feeling uncomfortable.

'As you described it, that should have been a very grievous wound. And you say you were able to hurt the abbot too?'

'Yeah. He bled.'

'Interesting indeed. I haven't come across anything like this in my research. Of course, I haven't met anyone who has survived a full-on encounter with whatever it is that ails Bailey. You, my young friend, are very interesting.' Naylor smiled at Josh. 'Let me feed you breakfast, eh?'

Naylor got up and started to bustle about the kitchen. Josh took a last sip of his tea. He was feeling a lot better.

'Thanks, but I'd better get back. I want to make sure Kate's safe.'

Naylor put bread in the toaster. 'Surely, just a piece of toast? You must be hungry?'

Josh shook his head. 'No, thank you.' He stood up and winced a little.

Naylor came over and put an arm around him. There was an odd smell off him, like stagnant water. Josh leaned away.

'Come now, let me help you. Don't be silly.'

Josh stepped away. 'I'm fine.'

Naylor took a step closer. He raised his bony hand and rested it on Josh's shoulder. The movement wafted the smell of filth towards Josh and with a shock he recognised it as the smell of thing which had pretended to be Kate.

'Of course you are,' Naylor said. 'I'm sorry.'

He stroked the back of his fingers across Josh's cheek and Josh jerked away. The fingers felt wet and he scrubbed at his face, wiping away something foul.

'Don't do that,' Naylor said. 'I don't mean you any harm.'

Josh put his hands out. 'I'm going now.'

'No,' Naylor said. 'I haven't had any company for a long time. Don't go. I just want to spend some time with you. Can't you let me do that?'

Josh backed up towards the door, watching Naylor. He tried the handle, but it wouldn't open. He fumbled with the key but it wouldn't turn in the lock.

Naylor grabbed him from behind and swung him around. His face was different. He thrust his fingers into Josh's hair. Josh put his hand on his chest and shoved him backwards.

Naylor's face twisted. 'Do what you're told, there's a good boy.'

Josh shook his head and Naylor rushed at him. Josh pushed him again. But Naylor was stronger than expected and clung to him. He pushed his face in close to Josh's. Josh put his open hand on Naylor's face and pushed with all his might. Naylor staggered backwards and fell to the floor.

Josh tried the key again. This time it turned. He rushed out and ran down the stairs, tearing the borrowed shirt off and throwing it on the steps.

He had to get back to the cottage.

Gabe sat up in bed. He had to see Kate. He got dressed fast and looked around sharply as the door opened. Darkness swarmed around him and he was blind. He felt a hand touch his arm.

'Gabe,' a voice whispered.

'Kate? Katie, is that you? What the hell are you doing here?'

He felt her arms come up around his neck.

'Gabe, I'm sorry you had to wait so long.'

'Kate, what are you doing?' Gabe heard the tremble in his voice.

She pressed herself against him and he put his arms around her. She was so slender. She felt so delicate in his arms, but he knew she was strong. She buried her face in his neck and he felt her breath on his skin.

'Oh, Katie,' he whispered. He relaxed and turned to her.

He found her face with his hands and kissed her. She was everything to him. She kissed him back with a fervour that made him dizzy. She was frantic, pulling him down onto the floor and he went, unable to think.

His heart was thundering and his breath was coughing out of his lungs, burning him. He felt like he had inhaled flames. His body pounded with his heartbeat and his muscles strained. They crashed against each other and the sound of it was like the crack of lightning. Gabe's eyes were open in the dark but all he could see was the pulsating red of his blood. Blackness squeezed his vision and the red faded to nothing.

When he came to, his body was prone and his arms were outstretched. His first breath hurt his throat and he groaned. He began to get up and pain shot through him. His arms were burning and his lower back was hot agony. He managed to get himself into a sitting position with his back against the wall. There was no sign of Kate. He shook his head and even that hurt. He felt whiplashed and beaten and the pain in his back was terrible. He got to his feet stiffly.

He had to get to Kate's. He didn't know what the hell had just happened but, if he was this bad, he didn't see how she could be OK.

He went downstairs and stopped outside the house.

'Gabe. You know that wasn't Katie,' he said aloud. The sound of his voice shocked him.

I know. That wasn't Kate. I know.

She wasn't safe. He had to get to her.

Chapter Twenty-five

Kate finally made it to the last piling. The water level was low here and she looked at the expanse of slick mud ahead of her. The bridge was above her. She swam through the last of the water until her hands and knees were lodged in the mud. She stayed still, resting. When she tried to pull her hand out of the mud, it sucked at her. She hauled her arm backwards and it pulled free with a loud slurp. She pulled the other hand free and stayed on her knees. She was about to try to stand when she heard a voice. It was very faint but it was definitely a woman's voice, soft and rhythmic. Kate felt a shiver run through her whole body, raising goosebumps.

There was something coming towards her, clinging upside down to the underside of the bridge. It was a girl, hanging upside down. Her hair hung down and she was twisting her body to look at Kate. Kate couldn't look away from her but her peripheral vision detected other movements under the bridge, approaching. There were whispers and scratching noises.

'*Child!*' The girl reached her arms out to Kate, smiling.

Kate struggled desperately towards solid ground. As she pushed with her feet, her sneakers were pulled off by the sucking mud – she left them behind her and struggled on. She clawed scoops of jellied mud as she went. A wet rotting smell rose around her. Sweating and nearly crying with effort, she pulled herself higher up the mud bank and into the sunshine.

Looking back, she saw the girl come to the edge of the bridge but stop there. Others began to crowd around the spot and Kate saw their avid faces staring after her. Turning away, she reached out, looking for something to grip. Her saw what looked like a fallen tree branch covered in mud but, when she touched it, it moved. She screamed and pulled her hand away, looking around her.

She was completely surrounded by thick eels, covered in mud, lying together on the bank. The smallest of them was thicker than her leg. They covered the mud entirely. There was no clear path to the grassy bank. She started to get up and the stinking mud tried to hold her. She lunged out of it and her foot came down on one eel. It lashed away from her and came to rest on the back of another one.

Kate froze, but the others remained still. She had been cold in the river but now a dead heat rose around her, baking off the creatures' backs. Flies buzzed around her face. Holding back a cry of disgust, she put her foot in a tiny gap between two of the thick bodies and stepped forward. The tough skin touching her ankle made her want to scream. She gradually picked her way closer to the shore. She was aiming for a rock which was sticking up out of the mud. If she could get to that, she could jump to the grass.

She placed her foot down again between two still eels and felt a smaller one squirm under her. She shrieked and pulled her foot back. The eel sank its teeth into her foot and she pinwheeled her arms in a desperate attempt to stay upright. She plunged backwards and felt the eels lashing under her. She tried to get up but everywhere she put her hands, eels were moving and writhing and she couldn't push herself up. She tried to keep her head up and saw a huge eel raising its thick ugly head out of the mud to loom over her.

Josh walked fast, figuring that when he loosened up he would jog the rest of the way to Kate's house. The day was warm enough to make being shirtless not too strange but he still felt uncomfortable. An old woman gave him a disapproving look as she went by.

He turned the corner at the end of the street and bumped into a guy standing there. There were others with him and, as the one Josh had bumped into turned around, he saw that they had blood on their hands and faces. Josh took a step around them but the guy he had bumped grabbed his arm. His face was twitching and his lips kept snarling back from his teeth and gums. Josh wrenched his arm away and stepped off the path onto the road. Two of the others stepped down and blocked his path. They looked to the first guy and waited. He came around in front of Josh and pressed his bloody and broken fingernail into his chest. Josh knocked his hand away. The others crowded around and Josh knew he was in real trouble.

Some women were at a vegetable stall in the middle of the wide path. Josh met one woman's eyes but she turned away, dragging her friend with her. He wouldn't be getting any help from anyone.

The guy put his hand on Josh's chest again, stroking him slightly and leaving a bloodstain on his skin. He nodded to the others and three of them lunged at Josh. He got a few punches in, but they didn't seem to feel them.

He was hauled up into their arms and, still silent, they carried him across the street along the promenade to the end of the bridge. Then they put him down. Josh backed away from them onto the bridge. They followed him, pushing him along the path. There would normally have been people and cars around at this time but the bridge was deserted. There was no one to help him.

The boys stopped close to the centre of the bridge. Josh stood facing them. Their leader grinned at him, head on one side, then turned and walked back along the bridge. The others followed. They all stood at the end of the bridge, not looking at Josh but forming a rough barrier.

Josh heard a noise behind him and spun around. Coming from the far side of the bridge was a giant stag.

It was breathing hard, its sides heaving in and out. He stood in close to the railing as it thundered towards him. It was pursued by a pack of men and boys with hounds. The hounds snapped at the stag and surrounded it. Josh was trapped by the stag, its flanks swinging around and pressing him against the rails. The hounds held it at bay. They were focused only on the stag but, as Josh tried to get away, he brushed against one. It shook its head and snarled and snapped at him. He twisted back, its teeth just missing him. One black beast next to him turned its head and looked at him. One by one, the human hunters turned towards him. He moved backwards until he was against the railing again. The nearest boy, teeth bared, took a step towards him in an attack crouch.

Josh, without taking his eyes off him, pulled himself up onto the rail and fell backwards as the boy leapt for him. He was at the highest part of the bridge when he fell and he plunged deep into the water.

When he surfaced, he was winded but close enough to the piling to grab on and get his breath back. Nothing had followed him into the water. There was no sign of hound or hunter. He swam under the bridge and struck out for the far bank. He couldn't go back towards town. Glancing over his shoulder as he swam, he couldn't see anyone watching him from above.

Then he saw someone struggling on the bank. When he got closer, he realised that the person was crawling into a mass of giant eels lying in the sunshine. He swam faster but the current seemed to be stronger here and it was hard to keep a straight line.

He came out downstream and struggled onto the mud. It was studded with rocks and he managed to get up onto the bank. He ran across the bank and jumped onto a rock sticking out of the mud. The person, a girl, had fallen back onto the eels and one was leaning threateningly over her.

Josh leapt from the rock. He struck the creature sideways and knocked it away from her. Its body was so thick that he was able to stand on it and grab her hand. He turned and pulled her half onto his back, lunging out and stepping on eels in huge jumps. He got back onto the rock and threw himself at the grassy bank, falling as he did.

The girl was crying and wiping the mud from her face.

'Kate! What the hell?'

Kate threw her arms around his neck and Josh hugged her. He helped her to her feet and they stumbled away, arms around each other.

Chapter Twenty-six

Richard's head was going to burst. The pain was almost constant. He often looked at Alma but she seemed almost deliriously happy. She didn't seem to be in any kind of pain at all. The buzzing in his head made it hard to think. He hadn't been home since she came to him yesterday and had cancelled all his patients. His secretary had argued but eventually had gone home in a huff. He had given Lynn some excuse about an emergency. Some part of him knew that she didn't believe him but he couldn't get up the energy to do anything about it.

As the hours passed he felt at times as if he was waking up from a nightmare, but when he did Alma was always still there. She sometimes went into dazes while he was looking at her, murmuring the name Josh to herself. She called him Josh at times as well. Richard felt lost and confused.

He was still sitting in the surgery at his desk as day dawned.

She walked over to him slowly, her hands on her hips in a parody of a sexy walk. She came around the desk and swivelled his chair so that he was facing her. She ran her hand into his hair. He closed his eyes and didn't move. She took his glasses off and threw them on the desk. She took his hands and put them on her hips. She leaned down over him and he smelt her breath on his face.

She put her arms around him and held him against her breasts. He was so tired that he put his head on her shoulder. When she let him go, the headache was back and he couldn't remember what he had been thinking about. He struggled to find it but it slipped away from him.

Some time passed without Richard really feeling it. He remembered the sensation of her putting her hands on him again and the phone rang a few times. When the sun was fully up, she began humming to herself, some classical piece that he couldn't place.

Then she stopped suddenly and came over to him.

'It's time now.'

Richard stood up and looked at his chair and his desk. He wanted to touch them. He gripped the corner of his desk as she grabbed his arm. She was massively strong and pulled him bodily away from the desk. He grabbed his glasses and put them on. He pressed his hand against his temple to stop the pain of his headache from bursting out through his skin. She led him from the office and

167

after a while he was aware of walking along the towpath beside the river. He wished it would rain. The heat had to break soon. He couldn't stand it. The cottage was ahead. It was friendly and homey.

Home. Richard frowned. Something about home. He really needed to be home. He came to a stop and Alma jerked his hand to make him start walking again.

She walked up to the house without hesitation and knocked on the back door. The girl's voice asked who it was. Alma dug Richard in the ribs and he said 'It's me'. The voice didn't sound like his own and he heard the locks being pulled back inside. When the door started to open, Alma hit it with her shoulder, driving it and the person behind it into the room. She flew in, carried by her own momentum and weight. Richard stood in the door, watching. She fell on the girl who had opened the door. She had stumbled back and Alma took advantage of her being off balance and pulled her into the sitting room and threw her on the sofa. She stood over her with a rock in her hand that Richard didn't know she had. The girl's hair was wet and she was dressed in a white blouse and jeans. She lay still on the sofa.

Richard felt something shift inside him.

'Get over here. Don't let her move.'

'OK, Alma.'

He went over to the sofa and took the rock. He stood over the girl and her eyes flicked to him for a second before going back to Alma.

Alma stared at her, then pulled her into a sitting position, digging her nails into her shoulders. The girl

168

winced then clamped her lips together.

'Where is he?'

'Who?'

'You know who. You think you can keep him from me, but you're wrong.' She slapped the girl across the face and her head rocked against the back of the sofa.

'He left. He won't be coming back.'

'*You're lying!*' Alma screamed into her face. She grabbed her shoulders and shook her like a rag doll before throwing her back onto the sofa. Then she began storming up and down the room, ranting.

Richard stood where he was.

'I know what's happening. Don't think I don't know. You knew I wanted him and you're keeping him from me. Well, I won't have it. We belong together. It's meant to be. I was told. He's to be mine always and I want him.' She leaned over the girl and shrieked into her face. '*I want him!*'

Kate hoped Josh would stay out the back where he was gathering wood to make a fire. They had both felt cold despite the warmth of the day.

'You can't have him,' she said.

Alma's big face turned purple. She stuttered an incoherent word into Kate's face and stormed away from her. She went to the kitchen and leaned over the sink. She got sick into it and young doctor Richard looked at her convulsing back with a sort of vague interest on his face. Kate had never been to see him but she recognised him from town.

Alma straightened up when she was finished and wiped her mouth on the back of her hand.

The door crashed open and Gabe burst in.

'Kate!'

Kate cried a warning as Alma picked up a wooden vase and lunged at him. He moved stiffly to avoid her. Kate tried to stand up, but Richard shoved her back onto the sofa. Gabe got an arm up to block some of the impact but the vase still struck his head. He fell to the floor. Kate cried out and tried to get to her feet again.

'Watch her, Richard, you fool!' Alma shouted.

Kate was pushed back again and then Richard bent over, pressing his hand to his temple.

Alma went into the scullery and crashed around in there. She came back with cable-ties and secured Gabe's hands and feet. She grabbed the ties around his wrists and dragged him over to the sofa with no obvious effort. She leaned over Kate again, baring her teeth. Kate felt her hot sour breath flow into her face.

'You better tell me where he is, but one way or the other *I will have him.'*

Josh put down the sticks and logs he had gathered and walked cautiously to the wall of the house. Something was wrong. He heard voices inside and moved along to the utility-room window. He waited. And then he saw a big girl pass the window, pacing. Alma.

He moved around to the front door and tried it. Locked. He moved a few flowerpots and found the key. He opened the door and started down the hall.

A man was standing with his back to the kitchen window, watching Kate. She was crouched over Gabe. He was tied up and looked semi-conscious. The man looked around and Josh recognised the guy who had thrown Kate in the river. They stared at each other for a moment before the man blinked behind his glasses. He looked over at Kate and Gabe, then back at Josh.

'I'm sorry.' He wiped sweat off his forehead. 'I'm sorry. I can't stop Alma. I have to go home now. My wife is having our baby.' His eyes cleared and he took a step towards Josh. 'I'm so sorry.'

'Oh! You're here.'

Josh turned. Alma was standing in the back door. She blocked the light from coming in.

'You came back for me.'

'Not for you,' Josh said.

Her face clouded over and Josh saw her shudder once before she rushed forward. She wrapped her arms around him and the speed of her rush knocked him backwards. She fell with him and knocked the breath from his lungs.

She lay half on top of him, crooning. She stroked his hair and ran her hands over his face. He managed to push her away and struggled to his feet as she grabbed at him.

Alma looked up at him from the floor. 'She said you weren't coming back. She lied to me.'

Josh stepped back out of her reach. She moaned and reached towards his leg.

Her accomplice leaned forward and put the heels of

his hands over his eyes. When he looked up, the whites of his eyes were pink.

Alma got up. 'You came back for me, not her. We're meant to be together.' She put her arms out to Josh.

He stepped further away and her face grew stormy again.

'You're mine. You're mine. I was told.'

'Never.'

She shrieked again and dived at him. He struggled against her but she was tremendously strong. Kate ran over and tried to get her off but she threw her elbow back and knocked Kate to the ground. Josh pushed Alma as hard as he could and she let go, taking a step backwards. She started to come for him again when the guy with the glasses ran at her and knocked her sideways with his momentum. She fell against the kitchen table, sending it skidding across the floor. She straightened up slowly and Josh saw her eyes change. They flickered as if a third eyelid had rolled up over the eyeballs and then slid back down again. They had a whitish cast to them as if they were layered with cataracts.

'Mine!' she whispered. *'Mine!'*

She started walking slowly forward and everyone took a step away from her.

Josh heard Kate say something and he looked at her quickly, not wanting to take his eyes off Alma for too long in case she came at him again.

'Kate?'

Kate had her eyes closed and she was praying aloud: *'The Lord is my shepherd, I shall not want. He makes me lie down in green pastures. He leads me beside still waters. He restores my soul.'*

Alma stopped and turned her white gaze on Kate.

'He leads me in paths of righteousness for his name's sake.' Kate opened her eyes. *'Even though I walk through the valley of the shadow of death, I fear no evil, for you are with me. Your rod and your staff, they comfort me. Surely goodness and mercy shall follow me all the days of my life.'*

Alma took a step backwards and stared at Kate. Josh took the opportunity offered by her distraction and stepped behind her. He grabbed her under the arms and, using all his strength, hauled her around, lifting her briefly off her feet, feeling his muscles creak as he did. He shoved her into the scullery and she pulled herself out of his grasp. She ran out the door, casting a look over her shoulder as she did, her eyes clear again. Josh could hear her keening as she ran towards the towpath, her flesh shaking on her frame.

'And I shall dwell in the house of the Lord forever ...' Kate's voice trailed away and she fell forward.

Josh leapt for her and caught her in his arms. He went down on to his knees and held her against him. He was barely aware when the man with the glasses came forward and touched his shoulder.

'My wife ... my wife is having the baby. I have to go. I'm sorry for ... I'm sorry for whatever happened. I didn't mean it.'

He backed away and, turning, left.

Josh helped Kate to her feet and she went to Gabe. While she was trying to rouse him, Josh shut and locked the front and back doors.

Kate wet a cloth and laid it gently against Gabe's head. He shuddered and opened his eyes. He sat up suddenly and then groaned in pain.

'Don't move, Gabe. You're okay,' Kate said.

She held the cloth to his head again. He sat still for a while.

'How do you feel?' she asked.

'Sick.'

'If he's feeling sick and sleepy, he might be concussed,' Josh said.

'I'll be fine,' Gabe said, his voice low and rough. 'I'm not concussed. I've had worse.'

Kate made a derisory sound and turned the cloth over to hold the colder side against Gabe's head.

'Don't worry about it,' Gabe insisted. 'I promise I'm fine.'

He started to get up and, despite his protests, Kate and Josh helped him onto the sofa.

'What the hell happened to everyone?' Gabe asked.

Chapter Twenty-seven

When Richard got home, Lynn flew into his arms and then slapped his face.

He told her over and over that he loved her. He didn't have any way to explain what had happened to him over the last couple of days, could barely even remember it. He wrapped his arms around her and put his hand on her bump.

'I'm not trying to keep anything from you. I feel like I was sick, or crazy. I don't know what happened. I just know how much I love you and I'm so glad to be home.'

Lynn looked at his face.

'Please, Lynn, trust me. I just want us to be together and to take care of our baby.'

Lynn put her arms around him and Richard took what felt like his first clean breath in a long time. She held him close and then he felt her stiffen against him. He looked at her.

'It's starting,' she said.

He helped her to get up and they looked at each other. Lynn was smiling and looking terrified all at once. Richard helped her to put on her shoes and timed her contractions. She said the pain wasn't too bad. He left her for a minute to put her bag in the car. When she felt okay, he helped her outside and into the front seat.

The pain started as he reached the main road. She screamed and a rush of bright red blood splashed onto her shoes.

Richard felt his face go cold. He put his foot down hard on the accelerator. Keeping one hand on the wheel, he lowered her seat to keep her flat. He felt around the back seat and found the car blanket to cover her. The blood kept coming.

He made it to the hospital in twenty minutes. She cried and begged him to help her most of the way. In the last five minutes, she fainted. He grabbed her wrist and he could feel that her pulse was racing hard. Her skin was sweaty and cold. The symptoms of hypovolemia from blood loss raced through his mind. He slewed the car sideways into a set-down-only area and ran into the accident and emergency room, screaming for help. He turned and ran back to the car with doctors running behind him.

He twisted his hands as they got Lynn out onto a gurney. He told them as much as he could and they took her away. He followed as far as the theatre doors and then slumped against the wall. A nurse tried to get him up and into a waiting room but he wouldn't move.

After a while, a nurse came and spoke to him and he followed her soft voice to a chair. A cup of tea was put in his hand, so he drank it. It was too sweet.

His knowledge tormented him. They would oxygenate her and give her blood and monitor her heart and brain function. And get the baby out. He knew everything that could be done and everything that could go wrong. He wished he didn't.

He had no idea how much time had passed but when they came to him he knew before they said anything that Lynn was gone. He looked at their faces as if they were speaking to him in a foreign language. It was both impossible to understand and somehow inevitable. He stood up and someone gripped his elbow.

They took him to see her. She was covered with a clean blue blanket in a clean white room. Her hair was damp and pushed back. Someone had washed her face. Richard sat down and held her hand. She was serene. He leaned close to her and saw a tiny spot of dried blood on her earlobe that someone had missed. He stared at it, hypnotised. He knew he had put that blood there with his failure. She had been taken from him because he had failed ... in something. He couldn't remember what.

He put his head down on her chest and lay there until another faceless someone came and took him out of the room. They made him sit down and then brought a baby to him. He looked at the little thing, all wrapped up, and didn't understand. Then they put the baby in his arms and Richard looked at his son. He held him and felt himself change.

Lynn was gone and now he was alone with this little person. Richard looked up at the window. Night had fallen since he had last been aware of the outside world. The moon wasn't full any more. Clouds passed across its broken face. He looked back down at his son. He had to protect him. He would do whatever it took to do that. Whatever it took.

Chapter Twenty-eight

Later, when everyone had cleaned up and Gabe had taken painkillers, Josh made sandwiches and tea. His muscles were sore from hauling Alma around, and the wounds he had received in the water were throbbing again so he took a couple of paracetamol with his tea too.

'The fact that no one would even look at you when the gang was giving you trouble is a bad sign, Josh. I don't think we'll be able to call on anyone for help.'

'What about Naylor? ' Gabe asked.

Josh hadn't told them about his experience with Naylor yet.

'I saw him this morning. He sort of attacked me, became someone else. Maybe he'll come out of it like the doctor but I'm not sure he'll want to be involved.'

Gabe took a deep breath. 'I think we also have to be careful anytime we separate. I thought I ... saw you ...

Kate . . . this morning. At my house. '

Josh looked at him. Gabe was staring at Kate.

'You came to see me. It was a fairly intense experience.'

Kate looked confused. 'What? This morning?'

Josh leaned forward. 'It was a fetch. Remember Naylor told us about them. It happened to me too. You came to me first, Kate.'

Gabe clenched his fists. Josh raised his eyebrows at him.

'It wasn't me either time and you guys getting mad at each other is insane!' Kate said angrily.

Josh made himself sit back in his chair. Gabe's jaw twitched as he ground his teeth but he relaxed his fists.

By the time dusk started to settle around the house, they hadn't got any further with deciding what to do.

Josh stood at the back door, listening to the sounds of the birds in the trees behind the house. Kate came up behind him and touched his arm.

He turned to her. 'I've been thinking. Maybe it would be a good idea for all of us to get out of town for a day or two to regroup. Clear our heads.'

Kate pursed her lips. 'Maybe, but it feels like running away.'

He nodded. She was standing close to him, her hair shining in the light from the kitchen He put one arm out and rested his hand on her waist.

There was a movement in the kitchen and Josh looked around to see Gabe standing there, his brows drawn together.

Kate looked at them both. 'But maybe it'd do no harm

for a few hours even, just for a break,' she said. 'My mam's car is here.'

'Can you drive?' Josh said.

'Yes, a bit. I'm insured on it and Gabe has his licence, so I can drive when he's in the car with me.'

Josh nodded. In lots of ways, Gabe seemed older than both him and Kate, and he looked older too.

They locked up the house, going out the back door. Kate unlocked her mother's little Fiesta, wiped away a cobweb from the steering wheel with a grimace before she sat in. Josh didn't like the way Kate smiled at Gabe as he got in beside her. He sat in the back, trying not to press into the driver's seat with his knees.

Kate was a bit shaky to start with but, after a couple of clunky gear-changes, she settled into it. She headed for the ring road around Bailey.

They were almost at the town limits when she slowed the car.

'What the hell?' Gabe said.

'It's just a checkpoint,' Kate said. 'We're OK.'

She pulled up beside the police checkpoint and started to lower her window.

'Wait!' Josh said.

The officer turned slowly towards the car. His eyes were glazed white. The colour of his irises showed like a bruise underneath the white. Two other officers standing by their car looked over and their eyes were blank in Kate's headlights.

'Turn around,' Josh said. 'We're not getting through here.'

Kate turned the car and the officers just stared as she did.

As soon as they were out of sight of the checkpoint, she turned down a back road and took them across country. When they were approaching the junction of the rural road with the main road, they saw that the exit was blocked by people.

'There's Alma!' Kate exclaimed.

She stopped the car some distance back from the junction. All of the people turned to look at them. Kate inched the car forward and the group took a step towards them.

Josh saw the gang who had forced him onto the bridge.

'I don't think we're going to get out of town tonight, guys,' Josh said. 'Let's just head back to the cottage.'

'Looks like we don't have a choice,' Gabe said.

Kate turned the little car on the narrow road.

The group stopped moving and watched as they drove away.

They got back to the cottage and parked the car. Everyone just sat still for a moment.

'I guess we stay here then,' Josh said.

'At least we're all together,' Kate said.

They got out and they all heard a noise from the river. A few drops of rain fell onto the dust of the lane.

'Is anyone seeing what I'm seeing?' Gabe said.

'Oh yeah,' Josh answered.

Coming around the bend in the river was a ship. It was a tubby ship with one mast and a square sail. There were men moving about on deck. She came to a stop and Josh could see a man standing at the bow. He walked forward to the towpath, aware that the others were behind him. A low mist crept onto the path from around the hull of the ship. He couldn't see the face of the man on the bow but he knew who it was all the same. He also knew that the ship was a cog and her name was *Zephyros*. The man on the bow turned towards him and raised a hand in greeting. Josh did the same.

He turned back to the others.

'Wait here. I'm going aboard.'

Kate put a hand on his arm.

'Josh, we should stay together.'

'I think he might be able to help us. Everything will be alright.'

He touched her face before turning away. He stepped into the low fog and felt the cold of it all through him. He looked back at the others.

'I'll come back, I promise.'

Gabe put his arm around Kate's shoulders and started to draw her away. She wouldn't move away but let his arm stay around her.

Josh walked further into the fog. He went to the edge of the towpath and stretched out his hand to touch the timber of the ship's hull. It was cool and rough. He grabbed a rope and pulled himself onto the deck. The shadows of the crew faded back to the stern and he walked forward to stand before the captain.

Halley wore dark clothes and had a light beard. His

face was kind and there were crinkles around his eyes, either from laughter or squinting into the sun, or both. He grasped Josh's hand and arm and they shook.

'You're Michael Halley.'

The captain nodded. He began to speak but for a moment Josh couldn't understand him. The captain stopped and took a breath.

'You're facing a difficult enemy. We have tried to defeat the abbot many times, you and I. He has grown strong on our defeat.'

Josh heard his voice and then an echo of his voice. He understood the echo.

'You and me?' Josh frowned but images started to come to him, crowding into his mind's eye. He remembered.

'And he takes a greater toll every time.'

This time, the strange doubling of Halley's voice merged and Josh understood him immediately. He knew that the abbot's toll was lives and souls.

'What can we do to stop him?'

The captain sighed. 'Have faith. Fight him. There isn't anything else.'

'Can you help us?'

'I will help you as much as I can. You have to go to the abbey and try to kill him. Keep your friends about you.'

Halley held out his hand and Josh stepped closer. The other man took his hand and Josh felt a surge of pain in his chest.

'I'll be with you now,' Halley said.

The light from the lantern intensified and turned red.

Josh staggered forward, aware of a sudden weight. The feeling gradually lifted and he straightened up. Halley was gone but Josh could still feel him.

He was back on the towpath and the cottage was ahead. The ship was gone and Gabe and Kate must have gone inside the house. Josh didn't know how much time had passed but the light seemed the same. His vision doubled for a second and he swayed. He pressed the heels of his hands into his eyes. It had rained and the smell of the earth was fresh and green. He walked slowly back to the cottage.

Kate rushed over to him when he walked into the kitchen. Naylor stood up slowly.

'Josh, I came to apologise. I'm not sure what happened.'

He came forward with his hand out. The man was as caught up in this as they were. It had been something else, not Naylor, sent by the abbot to torment him. Still, Josh felt his stomach lurch as he shook Naylor's hand. He sat down beside Kate, feeling heavy and tired.

'What happened?' she said.

'I spoke to him – to Halley.'

'So he's not dead after all?' Naylor said.

'He died but he's still alive. I don't understand how it all works.' Josh paused. 'He said I have to kill the abbot. It's up to me. He didn't tell me how.'

He would tell the others about Halley helping them, but he wanted to keep it from Naylor. He didn't trust him.

'I wonder if Mr. Ffrench would submit to hypnotism again. Perhaps we might find out the rest of the story from him?'

'Gabe, what do you think?' Kate said.

'Fine,' Gabe said, his face blank.

'Will you sit on the couch, please? Everyone else stay in the kitchen.'

Naylor sat on the edge of the coffee table and began to speak quietly to Gabe. Josh could barely hear what he was saying. After a few moments, Gabe sat up, his hands clasped between his knees.

Barron went out and hurried to Halley's ship. He climbed aboard, pulling his heavy frame up onto deck. He had a low feeling in his gut. He called Halley's name, surprised by the lack of volume in his voice. He cleared his throat and called again, but it made him feel wrong and out of place. He went below and found the captain's cabin. He pushed open the door and saw the dark blood pooled on the floor. Halley lay half out of the bed, reaching towards something not there. His throat grinned at Barron, white bone visible in the gash.

Barron had seen blood and death before in plenty. He wasn't revolted by it or its rusty smell. But he felt a surge of terrible anger force its way up his body. His face stiffened and reddened and he opened his mouth and roared his rage. He turned and blundered through the lower deck, reached the hatch and pulled himself up. He struggled back onto the dock, jumping the last few feet. With his heart pounding in his ears and his muscles popping, he ran for the tavern. He burst into the main room, startling the few remaining men to their feet.

'Halley's dead!' he roared. 'Raise the town!'

The others stared at him and he saw his own rage rise in their eyes. They ran, calling for their men as they did. Barron stood there, trying to breathe. He could hear angry voices and the thumping of fists against doors as the news spread.

Halley was well known and liked. No one even asked who had done the deed. They all knew. Soon, a huge crowd of people stood before Barron. A few of the men helped him onto a cask of beer and he used his biggest shipboard voice to tell them what he had found.

'They killed him on his own ship. His throat is cut and he's lying in his blood. He wanted to make peace. We all waited for him to come to make the peace and now he has been taken from us.'

The crowd roared. Barron stood silently, looking out across them. Torches blazed in the night and the smell of it burned his nostrils. He opened his mouth and roared his command across the quay.

'To the abbey!'

The mob turned and crowded up the quay to Sugar Lane. They passed the sugar stores with their heavy brown smell and burst out onto Abbey Street. The men carried torches and the women milled alongside them, screaming and enthralled. Ragged children raised from their sleep by the noise ran along the edges of the crowd. A few dogs barked and chased the children. The wide street led to the metal gates of the abbey and the crowd parted as Barron made his way through, cuffing people out of his way.

Torches appeared inside and the abbot came forward, the dwarf Long Pip at his side. He smiled at Barron, raising his *eyebrows in gentle enquiry. The dwarf grinned, his blackened teeth and gums showing.*

'Is my friend not with you, Charlie Barron?'

Barron snarled at him, his anger breaking. He ran against the locked gates, his big body making them rattle. The abbot held his ground, still smiling. But when Barron made his next run, the mob behind him ran forward too. There were screams of pain as some of them fell beneath the surging crowd but the gates began to give. The abbot's smile faltered and the dwarf turned and ran. The abbot looked around for support and found no one there. He took one last look at the crowd surging forward again and turned and ran for the building.

Barron crashed through the gates. Hands grabbed at him and held him up. He ran into the building after the abbot. There were cries of alarm from the friars within as they scattered in the face of the mob. Torches were thrown and wood and straw caught like tinder. The mob rampaged through the building, striking at friars where they found them. When the abbey was burning too much to stay inside, they dragged the friars outside and threw them to the ground. Barron emerged last from the building, his beard smoking. He clapped at it with one hand, the other hand grasping the abbot around the neck. He forced him forward and threw him onto the ground with his quivering men. The crowd grew quiet.

'The only thing stopping me from killing ye all is the memory of Michael Halley. He wanted to make peace. Get out of Bailey this night and never come back, the lot of ye!'

The crowd roared its disapproval but Barron screamed back at them.

'Bring them outside the town walls. Now!'

188

The crowd surged forward and many hands bore the friars forward. They carried them to the wall by the Marsh Gate and flung them onto the ground.

The abbot got to his feet and faced Barron and the mob.

'You don't know what you have done, Charlie Barron. You and this town will suffer for this forever.'

He paused and looked around at the crowd of now silent townspeople.

'You and all your children will suffer. You can have the town and the river. But I curse it, do you hear? I curse the river. From this night on, it will take its toll in blood.'

He turned and walked to the head of his band of friars. The mob watched them go. Frigid rain started to fall and when the friars were out of sight people began to slip away.

By the time Barron reached the quay, he was alone. He stood and looked into the water. The rain streamed down his face and the surface of the river was turbulent in the rainstorm. Barron shivered and went to claim the body of his friend. When he got to the cabin, the girl was there, cleaning the body. She looked up when Barron came in but didn't speak. The look on her face made him gentle with her. He helped her set things right. He needed to get her ashore. He had to find Halley's crew and get the ship to the centre of the river. Then when everyone was off, he would burn her. Halley had died for the town and Barron would do his damnedest to make sure that everyone remembered.

Josh watched Gabe get to his feet, his eyes unfocused. His face was twisted with grief. He looked around and saw the others standing at the door to the kitchen.

'We were friends once,' Gabe said.

Josh nodded.

'The river is cursed and the town with it,' Gabe said. 'How are we supposed to fight that?'

'We've fought it before, over and over. We just have to try harder this time.'

Gabe straightened his back and nodded. Josh walked forward, his hand out. Gabe took it. They shook and Josh's vision blurred so that he saw Gabe's face as it had once been: bearded and warm with friendship and respect.

He looked around at Kate.

'We're going to the abbey,' he said. They trooped back into the kitchen and Josh pulled black-handled knives from the wooden block next to the sink.

'Remember, these are only for your protection. I am going to kill the abbot if I can, but you guys just ... well, just take care of each other,' he said.

Gabe went to stand by Kate.

'We will. Let's go,' he said.

Chapter Twenty-nine

They got to town quickly. As they approached the bridge Josh put his hand out to them to wait and they stayed in the shadows while the bloodied gang of boys crossed over at the end of the bridge and went into town. They were silent and hunched.

When they were out of sight, Josh moved forward and went along the quay to Sugar Lane. They turned up the street and Josh became aware of a very strong smell from the old buildings. He looked up at them and the houses had transformed into small warehouses.

Kate looked at him, her face worried. She saw it too. It was starting. Naylor seemed lost in his thoughts, but Gabe followed their gaze.

When they got to the end of Abbey Street, the rows of houses had gone and the abbey stood there, looking strong and well cared for. Josh glanced at his friends and saw that they were dressed in simple rough clothes. Kate was wearing a long peasant dress, her hair in a thick plait

'Come on,' Josh said, pushing past Gabe to enter the abbey grounds.

As he did, the abbot appeared in the entrance to the building itself. Josh ran at him. The abbot disappeared into the abbey and Josh went after him. He looked around the great hall and couldn't see where the abbot had gone. There were monks standing around the edges of the hall, their hoods pulled over their heads. They began to close in. Josh could see their eyes glow white from under their hoods. He looked around and saw Kate and Gabe standing with him. Naylor stood back a little, looking frightened. Josh raised his knife. The others followed suit. The first monks came close and one grabbed Josh. Josh brought the knife down and felt it slip through the monk. His body disintegrated and collapsed on the ground, a puff of grey powder rising from his habit. A new wave flooded in behind him. Josh thrust the knife again and again. The others were doing the same around him. They were standing in grey dust as they fought and Josh heard Kate coughing. Two monks caught Josh's arms and started to drag him away, but Gabe lashed at them from behind, cutting their throats. They fell away from Josh and he was free. Kate was standing against the wall, her knife raised. Naylor skidded sideways to join them and pressed himself against the wall.

Josh turned when he heard Kate cry out. She was struggling and being dragged backwards into the wall.

Naylor grabbed her hand but Kate was ripped from his grasp and disappeared into the fabric of the building. Gabe slapped his hands against the wall, but it seemed solid. He turned to Josh, his face desperate.

Josh raised his knife, following an instinct. He sliced at the wall with it. It gave under the blade like fibrous skin and he forced the opening wider. It was dark inside but he stepped through and down.

Once inside, Josh moved aside to let the others follow. Gabe came last and stepped through backwards, his knife pointing at the monks outside who crowded up to the opening but didn't try to follow. When they all stood still, Josh couldn't hear a single sound. He felt like he had become profoundly deaf. After a long moment, he became aware of a sensation like a pulse. He couldn't hear it, but it echoed in his veins like a throb. His eyes became accustomed to the change in light and he realised he could see the shape of a great room. The walls were carved from rock and curved high over their heads. As he saw this, sound came back and he could hear the steady drip of water onto rock. A smell came to him too, of damp and darkness. He saw a movement to his left and looked down. A pale frog splashed into a dark pool and disappeared. There was a profusion of toadstools growing out of the rock, colourless and gelatinous. A lump fell off one and plopped onto the rock, still connected to its stem by a sticky thread of slime.

Josh moved forward, checking everywhere for Kate, in case she was injured and curled up somewhere. He was afraid of missing her in the dark. He stepped around the pools of water. They were black and it was impossible to tell how deep they were. The floor of the cave was sloping and he had to be careful not to slip. There was enough light to see but Josh couldn't figure out its source. The air was fairly fresh considering that they seemed to be underground.

Josh stopped suddenly, making Naylor walk into him and exclaim.

'*Shhh!*' Josh said.

The others stood still. Josh listened and then heard it again. A distant voice.

It was Kate.

'I can hear her. She's up ahead.'

Josh started moving again, faster this time. He slipped a couple of times, and saved himself by putting a hand on the cave wall. He scraped his palm and wiped it on his rough trousers. The ground began to slope more severely and then levelled out again. More water was dripping through the ceiling and they were soon walking up to their knees in it.

'We're under the river, I think.' Josh's voice echoed around the cave.

As they walked on, the tunnel narrowed and the ceiling got lower. The water level got deeper and Josh felt something move against his leg. He stopped and saw a huge white fish swim away. It was bloated and crawling with maggots where its back breached the water. He made his way to the side where the water was not as deep due to the curve in the floor.

'There's a ledge here. I think we could walk on it.'

Josh climbed onto the narrow ledge. Gabe shoved Naylor up and swung up himself, wincing a little as if his muscles were aching.

Josh started walking again. The tunnel started to turn and they followed the bend. It was a lot darker now and Josh walked with his hand on the wall. He rounded another curve and then his foot fell into empty space. He lunged forward and almost saved himself but plunged forward into the space, hitting cold water. He submerged and came back up without finding the bottom.

'*Stop!*' he shouted. 'There's a drop. I can't touch the bottom. I'm going to see if there's another ledge up ahead.'

Josh swam ahead, feeling the current tug at him. There was no ledge ahead on either side of the tunnel. He trod water for a minute in the dark, thinking. The tunnel was curving and they were probably in the middle of the wide river now. He reduced his movements to the smallest needed to keep him afloat in the undertow and listened. There was nothing at first and then he heard Kate's voice again, or an echo of it. It sounded very far away and distorted. She was saying his name.

Josh turned and swam back to the others.

'I can hear Kate again. There's no ledge. I'm going to swim. Do you want to wait here?'

'No way,' Gabe said and a moment later he was in the water.

'Doc, maybe you'd better wait for us,' Josh said.

'I'm a good swimmer, don't worry about me,' Naylor said.

A minute later, Josh heard Naylor lower himself into

the cold water with a gasp.

'OK, let's go.' Josh turned and swam ahead.

They swam in silence for a few minutes and then some ambient light made Josh aware of his surroundings again. His foot touched the bottom as he swam so he stood up. The water level was down again, reaching only to his stomach.

Gabe stood up and Naylor swam a little more before standing. Josh walked on as the water dropped away. He walked up onto a step and was back on bare rock. This cavern was smaller than the first one at the start of the tunnel. It was filled with strange light that made quartz in the rock shine.

The abbot stood on a raised table of rock in the centre.

Josh pushed his hair out of his eyes and went forward.

'Where is she?'

'Do you want her back?'

'Give her to me.'

The abbot laughed. It was a warm, friendly sound and it made the hairs stand up on the back of Josh's neck.

'I'd be glad to give her back to you, old friend. Once I've had my enjoyment. I told you what would happen if you persisted in opposing me.'

The abbot's smile faded and Josh saw a blurred image of the face under his skin. It was familiar and evil.

'I won't let you have her, Nicholas.'

'I keep my promises, Michael. I said I would take her and I have. You have only yourself to blame again.'

The abbot turned away and got down from the table of rock. He came to face Josh.

'She's mine now and I will take everything that you care about until you submit to me. She doesn't like anyone touching her, this one. Not like your serving girl, Michael, not as friendly by halves.'

Josh gritted his teeth and grabbed the abbot by his robe. He struck as hard with the knife as he could, burying it up to the shaft in the abbot's stomach. The abbot spun away and crashed against the table. He put his hand on his stomach and then held it up, showing the blood.

'It's good to bleed again, Michael. I was barely here before you came back. I have you to thank for my renaissance.'

The abbot straightened up.

'But unfortunately for you, your pitiful weapon won't work on me.' He rushed to Josh and leered in his face. 'I'm looking forward to enjoying my prize. If you stop now, I'll let you leave Bailey and you won't have to lose anything else.'

Gabe grabbed the abbot and spun him around.

'*Give her to me!*' he screamed. He punched at the abbot's face but the abbot seized him and threw him as if he were a rag doll. He crashed against the table. The abbot reached out and touched the stone table.

'This is where you will all lie when I'm ready to take you.'

The abbot waved his hand towards the table and Josh saw Kate writhing on its top. She turned onto her side and reached out. Josh leapt forward and threw his weight against the abbot, knocking him to the floor. The abbot shoved him off and stood up. Josh rolled and looked up at the table. She was gone.

'Do as you think best, old friend. I look forward to the game.'

The abbot faded and disappeared.

'Where is she? Help me find her! *Kate! Kate!*' Gabe ran around the cavern, while Naylor ran his hands over the stone table.

Josh knew that wherever Kate was, it wasn't in this place, at least not physically. He was burning inside. He didn't want to think of what might be happening to her, but images flooded his mind. He went to the table and stood up on it. The stone was darkened in places where blood had spilled.

Gabe looked over at Josh, his face fierce. Josh knew how he felt. He stared out over the cavern. He could feel Halley inside him and hear the sound of Kate crying. Josh barely knew who he was. He couldn't fight this. There was nothing he could do to save any of them.

Josh's idea, Halley's idea, had led to them losing Kate. There was nothing else he could do. And it seemed that the situation wouldn't even have escalated if he hadn't gone walking out the towpath and got involved with Kate and Gabe in the first place. He should have stayed with his parents after Callum's funeral. He shut his eyes and frowned. He had made things so much worse. If he left now, the others might be safe.

He jumped down off the table and went back to the tunnel. Gabe called after him.

'Josh. What are you doing?'

Josh stopped and looked back.

'I'm leaving. There's nothing else we can do.'

'*What the fuck?* Kate is here somewhere. We have to find her!'

'How? What do you want me to do?'

'I – I don't know. I just –'

'You want me to have some great idea that will bring her back. Well, I'm out of ideas. There's nothing left to do.'

Josh turned and walked into the water. Gabe splashed into the water behind him and grabbed his arm.

'You can't just leave her here.'

Josh shook his head. He pulled his arm back and punched Gabe hard in the face, catching his cheekbone. He fell backwards into the water, half blind and dizzy from the blow. Josh stood and walked deeper into the water until the bottom fell away.

After a few minutes, he heard Naylor follow him. He had a hollow cold feeling inside. He couldn't fight the abbot. Gabe called Kate's name over and over until he finally fell silent. He caught up with them by the time they got back to the first cavern.

They climbed through the hole in the wall and found themselves in the overgrown garden behind the houses. The sky was full of morning light. When Josh looked back, the wall was gone. Gabe walked past him, his head down.

Naylor left and Josh followed Gabe back to Kate's cottage without incident.

Josh sat at the table and Gabe leaned against the door.

'Is that it, then? You're giving up?' Gabe said.

'I'm leaving. That's what he wants. My parents are in Dublin. I'll go there.'

Kate will be safe if I go.

'Maybe. I'm going to keep looking for her.'

'I should never have come out here.'

'No.'

Josh shook his head. He had nowhere to go. It didn't matter where he was anyway. He couldn't escape himself.

'I'm leaving now.' Josh stood up.

Gabe followed him outside. 'You hurt her,' he said. 'I shouldn't have let you do that.'

Gabe put his hand on Josh's chest and shoved him back against the car. Josh felt anger rise in him and he was glad of it. It burned away a little of the hollow cold inside. He shoved Gabe back as hard as he could. Gabe swung at him and he ducked, punching Gabe in the stomach. The wall of muscles cracked against his fist and hurt like hell.

Gabe grabbed him around the shoulders and lifted him off his feet, throwing him sideways onto the side of the road. Josh lay in the dust and looked up at Gabe. All the anger washed out of him and he felt like lying in the dirt forever. Gabe was only doing what he would have done if the situation had been reversed. He didn't try to get up. Gabe kicked the dirt at him and went back into the cottage.

Josh painfully pushed himself to his feet and walked to the river. He stood on the bank and spoke aloud.

'*I'm leaving, Nicholas. Give her back. I won't oppose you any longer. Just give her back. Please.*'

Nothing happened. Josh turned and walked away.

Chapter Thirty

Kate felt arms going around her, pulling her. She struggled and fought, but whoever was pulling was too strong. The hands gripping her were so cold. She felt her arms going weak as she fought. She was starting to give up inside and letting herself be drawn backwards into darkness. She threw her arm out and banged it off the stone wall. The painful vibration echoed up to her shoulder and brought her back from the vague place she had been. She kept struggling and screamed for Josh. He was out there somewhere and she knew he would come for her. He wouldn't let her down. He would come.

She felt herself being pulled without effort. She felt like she was floating but she was dry. Unless she tried hard to control her limbs, they drifted against the flow of air sweeping past her like water. She tried to keep her head, looking about her. She was in a cavern and the stone ceiling was a long way above her. She cried out for Josh again and felt herself flung forward. She landed on a great slab of stone and was pinned there. It smelt like a butcher's shop. As she lay there, she heard the screams of those who had died on the stone block echoing through the granite to her ears. The stone felt warm and alive and it swayed under her like a gentle wave. She managed to roll to one side and saw Josh, Gabe and Naylor. She couldn't reach them. She started to sink into the stone and the world became dark. The last thing she saw was Josh's desperation and sorrow.

Kate sank slowly through the stone. She was drifting downwards for a long time and then she felt something grip her again. It was utterly without light but she was aware of the air being disturbed around her. She stilled herself, gathering all her energy and tried to lash out as hard as she could, screaming. She heard a chuckle in the darkness as her limbs twitched. A cold hand stroked her cheek and she sobbed, trying to twist away and not being able to. A finger scooped a tear from her cheek and then she felt herself being pulled again. Despair filled her heart and she closed her eyes. She tried to pray but she couldn't remember the words. Her lips moved but she couldn't speak any more. She retreated into herself, only one word forming in her mind. *Please.*

Barron disappeared into the ship and she hesitated, although she couldn't have said why. When he reappeared, he didn't see her, but went running back towards the tavern, his heavy body covering the ground faster than she thought he would be able to.

She walked slowly forward and climbed the gangplank. The ship was silent, except for the somehow sinister lick of water against the sides. She went below and found her way to the captain's cabin. The door was ajar. She pushed it open and stepped inside.

He lay in blood. His face was white and the rest of him was soaked in red. There was no way she could reach him without stepping in his blood, so she did. She went to him and touched his face. She closed his eyes and sat with him. She heard the noise from the quay as the mob gathered and later she smelt smoke, but she didn't move. After a while, she realised that she was the closest thing he had to a wife and that it was her duty to wash him.

All the time she washed him, she thought about how innocent her plans had been. She wanted to be with him for eternity. Instead, perhaps she could be with him in eternity. There was nothing for her here.

Barron came back and led her off the ship when she was finished.

She went back to the room she shared with the other girls and sat down. She wanted to die, but there was something stopping her. Sleep tried to claim her and after a struggle she let it.

She was on the Zephyros. The wind blew her hair back and the smell of the sea was as fresh as she dreamed it would be. Halley was waiting for her, smiling. She went to him and, when his arms went around her, she knew that she had been right. They would be together for eternity. He held her away from him a little and put his hand on her belly.

When she woke, she felt a little better. She would have to live for a while without him, but then they would be together again. There was a baby inside her to take care of until that time. A son of Halley's to carry his blood and his duty.

Kate woke up with her hand on her stomach. A son. She couldn't move. The dream faded and she remembered where she was. Trapped. Halley's eyes had been blue, like Josh's. The girl's name was Ellie. And she had a son with Halley. Generations of connection between Halley and Josh. Now, she understood how important Josh was to their fight. It was his blood and his destiny.

Chapter Thirty-one

He didn't go home. He just took the first bus out of town, following the great sweep of the road as it turned away from Bailey and from the river. He fell asleep and dreamt of Kate disappearing into the wall. She looked at him in desperation, asking for his help, over and over. He saw the disappointment on her face. He had made her trust him and then walked away.

Everything was wrong. He couldn't escape the dreams and kept returning to the cavern under the river, kept seeing the blood on the table, on the sacrificial stone.

When he woke, the bus was pulling into the terminal. He sat up, shaking his head. Something bad had happened. He frowned and shook his head again. He couldn't remember. He felt all damp and sticky. He walked a while for air, enjoying the fresh smell of the sea. He leaned on a wall and looked down. The estuary was below him. The scent of the brackish water came to him. Something echoed in his mind.

He raised his head.

What the hell are you doing?

He straightened up and everything flooded back. He saw Kate's face, betrayed. He heard her calling his name. He had to get her back. She was everything to him. He had to get back. There wasn't a bus but he had his emergency card with him and called a taxi.

The journey flew by and soon the downhill bend into Bailey was in front of him. The orange sodium lights of town were diffused by a mist coming off the river. He made the taxi driver take a roundabout route and drop him off near the woods. Once there, he made his way downhill to the cottage.

Why did Josh have to get involved? He had ruined everything and now he had abandoned Kate.

Gabe walked fast, feeling blind. He had loved her for years and now she was gone and this guy thought he was the one who was going to love her. It wasn't fair. He had loved her since they were children. She knew he had. Josh had only known her a few days. He couldn't know her the way Gabe did. It wasn't fair. He hated him. His vision blurred red as though blood had washed over his eyes. He hated him for taking Kate. And he hated her for the look in her eyes that should have belonged to him.

He banged his fists on his thighs and felt his breath catch in his chest. Anger flooded out of him and left him trembling. Her face seemed to hover before him. Her sweet face. He didn't hate her. He loved her. He sat on the edge of the dark towpath, not caring that he was close to the river, and wept painful tears, the first since his father died.

After a few minutes he tried to wipe the tears from his face and pressed his hands against his eyes. Pain welled in his chest and it was hard to breathe. He forced himself to take a long breath and then exhale it as he tried to get control of himself.

Then he heard a rustle from the river bank and something black leapt at him and wrapped itself around his upper body. He struggled with it but it clung on. He buried his hands in its crackling skin and tried to rip it from his face. He couldn't breathe and he couldn't prise it off him. He struggled for long minutes, scrabbling at the creature. It pushed him down onto the path, pressing the last of his breath from him. He blacked out with the foetid miasma of its body the only thing in his lungs.

When he came to, he struggled and fought against nothing. He couldn't remember what he had been fighting, but it didn't make any difference. He knew it was something to do with Josh. He could see them together, Kate and Josh, touching each other.

Everything had been fine before *he* had turned up. Gabe had been patient, waiting for her, being her friend, allowing her to find her way to him. And then *he* came and pulled her from the river and she started looking at him as if she had suddenly come awake.

Gabe looked at his hands. He knew what they could do. He was strong. He knew what his hands had to do for him and Kate to be together. He had to seize what belonged to him and claim it forever.

He went back the way he had come.

Chapter Thirty-two

Richard had stayed with the baby for a long time. He had taken care of him and sat looking at him for hour after hour. When he finally stood up to go, blood rushed back into his legs and he had to lean against the wall until the pain passed.

Then he told them at the nurse's desk that he would be back. He couldn't listen to what they were saying, so he just walked out of the hospital and drove home to Bailey.

A mile out of town, the car coughed and the engine cut. He was glad. Her blood was everywhere and he was close enough. He managed to get the car to drift to the side of the road and sat for a minute looking at a few drops of rain hitting the windshield. A roll of thunder sounded in the distance.

Richard got out and walked away from the car, not

bothering to lock it. He walked the last mile with only the moon for light. The streetlights lining the sweeping entrance to town seemed to be out.

When the road converged with the river again, Richard knew what he had to do.

Adam came awake suddenly. He was lying on his back in the wet grass of the park, staring up at the clouds and the moon. He was soaked. It must have rained on him. He lifted his head and felt the muscles in his neck cramp. He dropped his head back into the grass. A little later, he carefully hoisted himself onto his elbows and looked around. The other guys were lying on the grass as well. They looked to be still out.

Adam sat up and waited to see if he was going to be sick. His stomach roiled but then settled. He was starving. He rolled onto his knees and stood up. He nearly fell over Mark's feet and the idiot didn't even move. He gave him a kick and his leg moved with the force of it and settled back where it had been. Adam shrugged and winced when it hurt. He put his hand up to his neck and saw that he had blood caked on his fingers. He felt himself all over and, apart from aches, found no injury. Some small part of him wondered what had happened, but then he shrugged again and walked towards the entrance, leaving the others where they lay.

When he stepped out of the park, he looked back and could see only trees. He crossed to the river and went to the riverbank. He put his hands in the water and rubbed at them, picking the blood out from under his fingernails, letting it wash away into the dark river. He stood up and looked around. A few drops of rain fell on his face.

The town looked all wrong. There were only a few lights and no cars and too many trees. He walked out onto the road and couldn't see any way back into the park. He began to walk towards town.

When he got close to the quay, he could see ships moored along its length. Sailing ships, lots of them. This was definitely weird.

Adam walked along the waterfront, looking at the ships. There were a few guys around in rough clothes loading and unloading stuff. The place smelt of animals. Adam turned to cross the road and saw a lot of thatched houses. He stopped, frowning.

Where the hell was he? What was going on?

Alma felt she had a real purpose for the first time in her life. She held herself straight and smiled proudly into the mirror. She had someone now. She knew the most important thing in life was to have someone to live for. She would save him from the world and they could be together always. This world was just ashes. He would love her spirit as she loved his. And they would be safe from those who would try to stop them being together, those who were jealous of their epic love. She took a deep happy breath and went to get ready.

Naylor felt the aches of age touch his joints. He sat in his apartment in the dark, thinking. He remembered the pass he had made at Josh very well, but from a distance somehow. He had been celibate for many years, half through choice, half from lack of opportunity. He would never have made such an overt pass, even at a boy as beautiful as Josh was. Something had come from inside him that he hadn't known was there. He hated the horror and rejection on Josh's face but, at the same time, the image of Josh's face so close to his own sent a thrill through him. His clear skin and the blue of his eyes, even full of anger, were enough to stir feelings in him that he hadn't had for a very long time. Perhaps not since those days when he could discuss poetry and history with those wonderful eager boys in the university, discuss the great moments in the story of the world that meant so much to him. Long nights full of conversation and the smell of hash, where he sat as a guru on cushions and held them rapt.

He couldn't understand where those times had gone. He still felt like the same person. And now, this glorious boy had come along, bursting with the same possibilities of conversation and hope. And he had almost ruined the chance of observing him, of watching his mobile expressions, the way he ran his hand through his untidy hair, the way his lean body moved, muscles tensing and releasing under taut skin. Had almost lost the chance of being close to him, smelling no aftershave or perfumes, just the fresh scent of youth and beauty.

He stood up and went to the window. The moon was going in and out between clouds and making the street dark and light in harlequin flashes. Naylor felt stifled by the apartment and wanted to get out. He pulled on a cardigan, grown long with age, and left.

213

Chapter Thirty-three

Kate opened her eyes and looked into the dark water. She was frozen in a twisted position. Her legs were lying at an awkward angle and her left arm was thrown out to the side. She could move her head but nothing else. She was wet but not in the water. When she looked up, she could see the surface of the river far above her and the moon appearing and disappearing.

She looked again at the river and saw a huge eel swim close to her. It turned its head and snapped at her casually as it passed. Its teeth didn't touch her. It was followed by others, large and small. They circulated around her, never touching her. She could feel their movement washing her from side to side. She looked down under her outstretched arm and saw the muddy bottom of the river below her. A spar of a ship poked up out of the mud. A fish swam around it and one of the eels snapped out of formation to snatch it. Another eel came to the edge of the pack to take its place. It had a small foot in its jaws. Kate screamed but couldn't hear herself. She kept struggling and calling Josh's name. This was her nightmare and she wasn't about to give up.

Chapter Thirty-four

Alma stepped outside her door. She felt like she could walk a thousand miles. Her body was nothing, compared to her desire. The night was heavy with the prospect of thunder. She was glad. She didn't want any more heat. When the storm came it would clear the air. She strode out into the street, aware of herself, a big girl taking up barely enough space to accommodate her great spirit. She was immortal. She and Josh were Isis and Osiris. They had been separated but soon would be together for always. She felt so strong. She would claim him and he would look at her with that timeless love that would transform her into the beauty that she knew she was by right.

The town was different. It didn't matter. Everything was different now. She plucked a loose piece of straw from a low thatched roof and threw it into the night sky.

A whisper of a breeze took it and Alma felt like she could fly with it. She went out to the centre of the bridge and looked out over the river. The moon showed itself and glittered on the surface of the water. It was beautiful. Alma wanted to go into the water. She put her foot up on the timber rail and then frowned. That wasn't right. Not yet. She had to get Josh. It wasn't right without him. She laughed at her foolishness and patted the bridge with affection. Not yet. She turned back and walked along the quay, waiting for the right feeling to tell her what to do.

She sat down on a pack left over from the unloading of a ship and waited. After a few moments, she heard someone coming. She looked up and nodded. This was right.

Richard stopped walking and looked at her. She stood up and held her arms out. His face didn't change but he walked forward and she wrapped her arms around him. He had been sent to help her.

Richard turned and walked back along the quay. Alma followed him. They passed an old man standing at the water's edge. He shrank back as they went by him, terror on his face. Alma smiled. This was another sign of her incredible power. Ordinary people were frightened of her. The setbacks of the past were over. This time, nothing would stop her.

Richard walked up to someone and put his hand on his shoulder. The boy turned around and Alma saw blood on his face.

Gabe got back to Kate's cottage. Once inside he stood in the dark hallway at the bottom of the stairs. The house seemed to echo with the ghosts of his memories of Kate.

After her father died, and her mother went crazy, no one seemed to care. She was just one more person in trouble in Bailey. But Gabe had cared. He had read that once you save a person's life, that you're responsible for them forever. Gabe's own father was dead and his mother was weak. There was no one to care if he stayed out late or didn't come home, or used his size to start fights and end them. Except Kate, who always told him off for getting into trouble.

When trouble had come to her door, she had spent months eking out an existence on her mother's savings and somehow managed on her own.

Gabe closed his eyes and saw her.

She gave him the ability to be everything that he could be. Her eyes were enough to tell him. They were as bright as they had ever been, but there was something old behind them now. Her face had thinned over the last few months, maturing into beauty. But the soft expression of the girl he had known was there when she smiled. Gabe did everything he could to make her smile.

They had one night that was close to being a date but when he tried to kiss her, she turned her face away. He knew that she wasn't ready. And now, when waiting was supposed to bring him the prize, she had turned away from him again. And into the arms of someone else. Someone not worthy of her.

Gabe ran his hand over his face. He started upstairs and went to her bedroom. He wanted to be close to her things.

He held her pillow against his face and breathed in the scent of her, then sat on her bed, holding the pillow. After a while, he went back downstairs and out the front door. The air smelt like a storm was coming. The scent of honeysuckle from the wood was heavy. He went out onto the towpath and looked up into the trees. Josh was up there somewhere, trying to take Kate away from him. He was going to stop him for good.

Chapter Thirty-five

Josh went outside and locked the door. A few drops of rain hit his face, fat and slow. Thunder rumbled higher up the valley. He walked out to the edge of the path and saw movement in the darkening river. Multiple ripples covered the surface of the water, becoming eruptions as something under the surface convulsed. A body emerged from the water in a burst of air or gas. The person struggled on the surface. The man turned to face him and he recognised him from a picture in the cottage. Kate's father.

Josh looked back at the river. The man was moving through the water as though slowly propelled. He grasped at the grass on the bank and pulled himself out. He was covered in greasy mud. His left arm was gone and the side of his head was a mutilated mess.

'Josh.' The voice was filled with mud. 'You lost my

little girl,' he crooned, 'but she's here with us now.'

Josh looked back at the river. The whirlpools were disgorging other bodies which were flooding towards the shore. They began pulling themselves onto the bank. They were all ruined in one way or another. Some of them were bones covered with mud and algae, some were intact but terribly white. They crowded around each other on the bank. Two of them stepped forward and stood to one side of Kate's father.

Josh's heart lurched as he recognised them. He reached slowly up and slapped himself on the cheekbone that Gabe had punched.

'*It's not them*,' he said aloud and stepped backwards.

Kate and Callum slipped their arms around each other.

Josh turned his face away and saw that the river's surface was still disturbed by more bodies erupting from the muddy bottom. The moon emerged from the clouds and Josh could see the river all the way to the bend. There were bodies thrashing across its entire surface. The towpath was crowded with the river's dead and more were scrambling over each other to pull themselves up.

'Josh!'

Callum's voice made him look again. They were walking towards him. Callum looked perfect, normal, his big brother. Except for his eyes which were empty, dark sockets.

Josh jumped down into the dyke beside the towpath, skidding as he landed. The rain had filtered through the canopy to make the earth slick. He slipped on moss and

221

flattened weeds. He climbed over a fallen branch and started away again but slipped again and fell hard, cutting his arm on a spur of a broken branch. He looked back and saw them coming, the dead of the river.

Josh scrambled up and ran as fast as he could, ducking under branches that clung to his clothes and slapped at his face. He went higher and the climb became harder. When it levelled out, he burst out into a clearing half covered by the great canopy of a huge oak. The moon came out briefly and showed him that the ground was moving. He was skirting the edge of the clearing when the first skeletal hand reached out of the wet ground. He plunged back into the woods and kept going, until he could hear nothing but his own breathing and his heart beating in his ears.

He stopped in a dark clump of young trees and listened. When his breathing calmed, he could hear that the wood was silent, except for the sound of running water from a stream somewhere close. He turned his head when he heard a branch cracking downhill from his position. He thought he saw something dark separate from the shadows down there. As he listened there was a rumble, a vibration felt rather than heard. A black creature was crouching on the ground below him. It shifted as Josh looked at it and made ready to spring. Josh waited until the creature jumped at him, then threw himself hard to the right. It struck the slender trees and crashed to the ground where he had been standing. Josh ran. There was no time for care and he broke through trees and undergrowth, shielding his face with one hand.

As he ran, he could hear the excited yipping of the creature following him, interspersed with growls each time it grew near. Josh kept turning and ducking between clotted growths of wild forestry. He was trusting entirely to fate, as the ground rose and fell unpredictably under his feet, but he was drawing ahead of the creature.

Josh ran over a rise and the ground disappeared, dropping from under him. He fell, crashed through some branches and landed flat on his belly at the edge of a stream. He got up onto his knees and heard the creature crashing towards him. He felt around on the ground and found one of the branches he had broken with his fall. He braced himself against a large rock on the bank of the stream and waited, listening to the creature rushing closer.

It burst through the gap Josh's fall had made and fell towards him. It spread its body like a bat and swooped down. Josh held the broken branch firm and it burst through the creature's chest, puncturing its skin with a pop. Its weight strained his muscles but he held fast, thrusting the branch upwards. The creature's body slipped downwards on the branch and a rush of fluid surged out of it and washed over Josh's hands. The creature struggled, impaled. Josh jerked the branch hard sideways. The creature slid off the branch with a scream and flew into the bushes at the far side of the stream. Josh stood up and waited but there was no movement from the other side of the water. He put his hands into the icy flow and washed off the stinking hot fluid. He dried his hands on his jeans, then jumped the stream, avoiding the bushes where the creature's body had landed.

He made his way forward more slowly, choosing his path more carefully. He came out onto another clear area. Moonlight showed him a deer standing in the middle of the clearing. She turned soft dark eyes on him before turning and walking to the far edge of the space. She paused and looked back at him.

Josh heard movement in the forest behind, quite far back. He stepped into the clearing and walked towards the deer. She went into the woods and Josh followed her. As he did, the noise of pursuit increased and Josh heard a deep howl, followed by the sound of a pack giving voice. The baying rose in the air, coming up the hill of the forest and making the hair rise on the back of his neck. The deer broke into a run and Josh followed her. She drew ahead, but Josh kept watching for the white flash of her tail. She sprang and bounded almost without sound, following an unseen path. The hounds pursuing them were bursting through the bushes and trees, baying and snarling.

They were flying through the forest, he and the deer. The woods were deeper than Josh had thought possible. Behind, Josh saw the first hound coming into sight, its red eyes burning. There were many others in the darkness behind and he thought he saw a man among them.

Josh looked ahead again, afraid to lose sight of the running deer. As he found her again, she took a sudden leap and flew, her slender legs tucked under her. Josh could only act on faith. He leapt into the darkness.

The forest showed the signs of intrusion. There were lots of broken branches and crushed undergrowth. Gabe followed the path carefully. He could hear something up ahead and he half walked, half climbed until he came to a clearing, highlighted by the flashes of the moon. The clearing and the surrounding woodland were full of people. He walked slowly among them. They stepped aside as he passed. He looked at their faces, at the devastation of their bodies. He walked to the centre of the grove and stopped, turning in a slow circle. They began to move closer to him and then dropped to their hands and knees. The moon came out and shone on them, on flesh and bone, on Gabe standing in their midst. They changed as he looked at them, bending and twisting, growing teeth and hair.

When they were all changed, Gabe turned towards the woods again and raised his hand. When he began to run, they followed him, baying.

Gabe ran through the trees, the pack at his heels. Some of them began to outpace him, howling. He felt them brushing against his legs, felt the waves of cold emanating from them. Some of them hadn't fully changed. Gabe saw one running on three legs, carrying a human arm across its chest. One was hairless across its back and down its side and he saw a woman's breast swaying from its chest as it ran. He turned his gaze back to the path and kept running.

Soon, he saw Josh ahead, running hard. Gabe kept on,

only vaguely aware that his lungs were burning and his muscles trembling. It was outside of himself. He kept his eyes fixed on the fleeing figure, a mere moving shape in the dark. Then it was gone.

The hounds kept running and disappeared, howling as they went. Gabe skidded to a halt, grabbing at a tree to swing himself to a stop. The hounds nearest to him stopped, but one teetered on the edge of a drop, its nails scrabbling against its momentum. For one moment, it seemed as though it would regain its centre of gravity but it tipped over slowly. Gabe saw it lose its hound shape and become human again as it fell. He walked slowly to the edge and looked down. The ground was creased by a fast-running stream, cutting deep into the soft limestone and soil. The gap was not wide but deep. Broken bodies lay at the bottom. Josh was not among them.

Gabe backed up and ran at the precipice, energy surging through his powerful legs. He came down easily on the other side and looked back. None of the hounds were coming.

He turned and listened. He could hear the distant sounds of fast movement ahead. He started after them.

The deer was gone. Josh stopped, his breath rasping. He listened to the forest. There was still something coming after him, but only one. He made his way off the rough path into a thicket. He scouted for a rock and found a hand-sized one that had been unearthed when a small tree had fallen in a storm.

He waited until he heard his pursuer coming close, then he leapt out, throwing his full weight against him, knocking him deep into the woods. The man got up quickly and sprang at him. Josh raised the rock and the moon filtered through the trees. He hesitated when he saw Gabe's face, his lips curled back in a snarl.

Gabe grabbed Josh's wrist and twisted his arm. Josh dropped the rock, but punched Gabe in the ribs, feeling the impact all through his arm. He knew that on strength and size that Gabe would win. He pulled his wrist free and dug his feet into the earth. He shoved Gabe in the chest and followed him, punching wherever he could land a blow. Gabe punched him on the cheekbone again and stars burst around him, but he kicked Gabe in the knee before he could come in hard.

Gabe grabbed his knee for a second but then came at Josh with his head down, bellowing. Josh grabbed him but Gabe's momentum drove his head into Josh's belly, knocking the air out of him. He caught a tree and pulled himself around in a half circle, so that Gabe's follow-through missed him. He put his fists together and brought them down on Gabe's thick neck as he passed. Gabe went down on his knees but rolled and bounced to his feet immediately. He came at Josh again and this time, Josh, taller and standing on a slight rise, hit him as hard as he could with his head. The pain and shock of it made Josh stagger to one side, but Gabe had gone down and rolled down the slope, then came to a stop and stayed still.

Josh put his hand to his forehead and wiped away blood. He didn't know if it was his or Gabe's.

He looked around until he found his rock and then waited.

After a few minutes, Gabe started to stir and Josh moved back a step. Gabe opened his eyes with a groan. He leaned on one elbow and spat blood. He heaved a very weary sigh and looked up at Josh, squinting.

'Hi,' he said. 'Sorry.'

'*What?*'

'I think I was ... not myself. I wanted to kill you. Something got into me. Some black thing.' He shuddered, looking sick. 'I guess you knocked it out with your rock.'

Josh swopped the rock to his left hand, but didn't drop it. He put his right hand forward and Gabe looked at it before taking it and letting Josh pull him up. He leaned against a tree.

'I would never hurt her,' Gabe said. 'We're going to find her and if you ever hurt her or abandon her again, I will kill you.'

Josh winced, then nodded. 'Fair enough.'

He looked up. The clouds were getting heavier and it was harder to see the moon.

'A storm is coming,' he said. 'Let's go up. I think we might come out near the town wall.'

He turned and started to make his way uphill through the trees. When he stepped out of the forest onto a dirt path he looked around to get his bearings and realised he was well outside the town wall. There was a group of low rough cottages ahead and the path led through them.

Gabe stepped up beside him and he nodded to him and walked towards the little village. The track was well worn but the edges of it were unkempt. They passed a rudimentary well with a jug of water sitting on its edge. Gabe reached to get it, but Josh grabbed his wrist and shook his head.

A little dog barked as they passed the first cottage and the door opened. A woman looked out at them in silence as they passed. A faint glow from inside framed her and they couldn't see her face. Someone in the little house opposite also came to their door and the light crossed the narrow space and showed them the woman's face. She had been ravaged by disease and was covered with open sores. She wore a simple garment that left her arms bare. She had material wrapped around some parts of her arms but wet sores were visible on the exposed skin. She looked at them with blank eyes. No one spoke. They went silently through the village and back onto a more open road.

'Leprosy,' Josh said.

Gabe swore under his breath.

The road widened steadily as they climbed another hill. A more established village came into sight with a very wide main street. The cottages were bigger and there was evidence of a market.

'This is Irishtown,' Gabe said, frowning.

Josh nodded. They were having impossible memories.

Josh kept moving. The Hart's Gate was ahead. The tower in the wall became visible against the sky although the moon was now covered. A few drops of rain began to fall as though dripping from trees.

Josh went through the gate. There was no one around to stop them.

Once they got inside the wall, the rain started to come down in earnest. They were soaked through in seconds. Josh slicked his hair back and shrugged at Gabe. They walked downhill towards the abbey. By the time they reached Abbey Street, water was running in streams past them. They could only put their heads down and keep going.

Josh looked up as they crossed the top of Sugar Lane. Through the veil of water, he saw that there were a few people standing outside the abbey. He nudged Gabe with his elbow. They hadn't been seen yet. Josh stood in against the wall of a merchant's house. He was about to speak into Gabe's ear when a figure emerged from the meagre shelter of a doorway and put his hand on Josh's chest.

Naylor looked thinner than usual, with his loose clothes plastered to his body by the rain. Josh grabbed him and pulled him in next to the wall.

'I've been watching them. It's a big woman and two men, one of them a boy really,' Naylor said, his mouth close to Josh's ear. 'The boy has blood on his face, or he did before it started to rain.'

Josh wiped water from his face with his sleeve. There were three of them against the three at the abbey, but Naylor didn't look like he would be much good in a fight.

He closed his eyes and thought about Halley.

The feeling of rain on his face went away. Someone was speaking but the sound was distant. Other sensations filled his mind. He could smell the sea and feel spray on his face. He felt the sway of the ship. The *Zephyros*.

C'mon, Halley, help us.

He waited but there was no answer. He took a deep breath and focused on the sound of creaking timbers, the cry of seagulls.

Halley, I need you. Tell me what to do.

When the answer came, it was more of a feeling than words, but the meaning was clear.

Go back through the tunnel. The Smugglers' Tunnel. Find the entrance. It'll lead you under.

Josh opened his eyes. He turned to Naylor. 'Do you know anything about smugglers in the abbot's time?'

'Ah, yes! I think there was a village across the river that harboured thieves and pirates.'

'Smugglers,' Josh said. 'They used the tunnel we were in before to come and go under the river. If we find the entrance, we can use it to get to Kate.'

He put his hands over his mouth and nose. The smell of the sea was still on his skin and, as he inhaled, a feeling of certainty rushed through him. He knew exactly where to look and what to look for.

He signalled to the others to follow him and started up Marshall's Hill.

The rain eased a little as they climbed. When they got to the top, Josh turned left and went into a small grove of trees. A stone cross stood at the centre of the grove.

'This is it. We need to dig.'

Josh looked about and found a flat stone with a sharp edge. He got down on his knees beside the cross and dug the stone into the soft earth. The others selected stones and started digging too. Soon, Josh hit more stone and they scraped the soil away until they could see that a square stone slab had been concealed. Together, they cleared the edges fully and managed to half lift, half slide the stone away, revealing a tunnel. There was a sound of running water. Josh dropped a stone and heard it splash into the water.

'I don't think it's too big a drop. I'll go down first and check it out.'

He sat on the edge of the hole and put his legs down, before turning around on his belly and letting himself drop back. He could put his feet against the wall inside and half sliding, half dropping, he let himself go into the dark.

The drop was only a couple of feet below him at his full length and he found himself standing on fairly flat ground in water that came to his ankles.

'It's OK. You can come down.'

Gabe lay on his belly and helped Naylor down. His knees gave as he landed and Josh grabbed him. Gabe hopped down easily, bending his knees to take the landing.

'Are you sure this is a good idea?' Gabe said.

Josh shook his head. 'I don't think I'm in charge anymore. I think Halley is helping us out. I say we go along.'

Gabe shrugged. Josh turned around and faced the tunnel.

'Everyone stay close. We're going to have to do this in the dark.'

Josh started forward, one hand on the side wall, the other ahead of him. He took a sliding step in the low water and moved slowly forward. After a few steps, he closed his eyes, then opened them and could detect no difference. He could feel a cool breeze on his face and they were obviously walking downhill. He asked the others occasionally if they were OK but otherwise they moved in silence. The side walls became gradually further apart and the water became a little deeper and faster. Josh was walking for some time before he realised that he could make out shapes. The tunnel became brighter and colder the deeper they went. Josh thought that they must be quite far below the surface and hoped that they were close to the abbey.

Josh became aware of the sound of rushing water ahead. It got louder as they walked until it thundered in the tunnel.

There was enough light from somewhere ahead to show Josh that the tunnel floor dropped out of sight. He stopped and told the others to wait before moving carefully to the edge and looking down. It wasn't a vertical drop, but rather a steep slope that ran at an angle down to join fast-flowing water in another tunnel. Josh couldn't see anything beyond the water at the end of the slope, but he had a strong feeling that they should go down. He called the others forward and they all looked over the edge.

The water they had been walking in was foaming

below where the two streams met.

'I'm going in. Anyone who wants to should turn back.'

'I'll try,' Naylor said. 'I don't know if I can do it, but I won't turn back.'

Gabe just raised his eyebrows at Josh and folded his arms. Josh stepped to the edge, sat down on the path and pushed himself off.

The water took him and he slipped onto his back. The journey down was fast and he barely had time to snatch a breath before he shot out over the edge, spent a second in the air and plunged into the icy water of the underground river. He kicked to the surface and tried to look back at the slope but the river swept him beyond the turn and sharply downhill. The water was white around him and he was glad it seemed deep and not rocky. He was thrashed by the current and was mostly blind to his progress. He swept around a quick series of turns where the river cut through softer rock. His leg hit the side and pain shot up through him. The river spun him and he saw the water redden briefly before he was swept onwards. He kicked around to face forward and saw the drop ahead.

There was nothing he could do. He kept his eyes open as he went over the edge and dropped. He fell free of the river and dropped like an arrow into a deep pool. Under the surface, he was spun around and he kicked as hard as he could to get clear of the vortex. He got to the surface and made it to the rocky side of the pool. He pulled himself from the water and sat on the edge. His calf was torn and blood ran in rivulets from the wound.

A scream echoed through the chamber and he looked

up. Naylor flew out over the edge and plunged into the water. Josh dived in, grabbed Naylor's arm and pulled him to the surface. He swam with the older man to the side and boosted him up onto the edge. Once Naylor was out, Josh waited for Gabe in the water, in case he needed help, but Gabe rose to the surface straight away and swam to the edge in two awkward but strong strokes. Josh followed him and got up onto the edge again. He looked at his calf. The water had washed away most of the blood and the wound looked raw but was only bleeding slightly. Josh stood up and tested his leg. It hurt some but it bore his weight.

He looked around at the cavern they were in. It wasn't as big as the central cavern where they had seen the abbot, but it spiralled high into a distant ceiling. The river continued on its way through an arched gap in the stone. There was a ledge along the edge of the river that they could use.

Josh pulled himself up onto the ledge and helped Gabe get Naylor up. They started along the ledge.

Very soon, the ceiling got lower and Josh had to bend his head to get through. The river ran fast beside them and the ledge was narrow, but they had no choice but to go down on their knees.

A grey light was visible ahead and Josh squeezed through a fissure in the rock. He was able to stand up on the other side. He was back in the central cavern under the abbey. The stone table stood in the middle but otherwise the cave was empty.

Chapter Thirty-six

Richard and Alma were standing outside the abbey.

Richard looked at Alma. Her eyes still showed the colour of her irises but they had started to cloud over. Her skin was pale but her cheeks were splotched with colour that looked like broken veins. Richard's headaches were gone but he felt a burning in his stomach that radiated pain into his chest. He often couldn't remember what he was doing here but then Lynn's face would flash into his head and he would remember that her death was all his fault for resisting, for failing. He saw the baby and moved his hand to cup his head and looked into his sleeping face. Alma dug her fingers into his arm and the image of the baby faded away.

Alma turned away from him and walked into the abbey. Richard looked at the boy who had joined them. Most of the blood was gone from his face but when he grinned at Richard, his teeth were stained with it. Adam, he said his name was. He followed Alma inside and Richard went after them, feeling an ache in his arms as though he were still holding the baby after many hours.

It was dark inside but there were a couple of torches on an upper level that shed some light into the hall. Richard looked around. There were monks standing there, their hoods pulled over their heads. Their eyes were opaque white. A small figure stepped forward and pulled his hood down. When his distorted face was exposed, Richard recognised him but didn't understand how he did. The dwarf walked up to them and pulled a knife from under his habit. He handed it to Richard and nodded, grinning crookedly.

Richard felt his hand go out and he took the knife by the blade. He jerked his wrist and the knife flipped and came back into his hand, fitting neatly in his palm as though made for him. The dwarf nodded and grinned again. He turned and walked back to the rest of the monks, not quite joining them but staying one step forward of the group, watching Richard closely.

Alma looked at Richard and waited. Richard felt heat in the haft of the knife and felt it pulling him. He walked across the hall and touched the knife to the wall. It slid through the stone like butter and the wall opened up to him. Alma, behind him, clapped her hands and shoved him out of the way. She climbed through the gap and the boy scrambled through after her. Richard followed them, feeling the knife warm and alive in his hand. Inside, Alma grabbed him and tried to shove him forward. He turned on her, the knife in his hand, baring his teeth at her. She fell back and the boy laughed, the sound echoing through the cave. Richard turned away and began to follow the heat of the knife.

Chapter Thirty-seven

'She's not here,' Gabe said.

'No, not here, but close.' Josh walked around the stone table in the centre of the cavern. He put his hand on the stone and felt it vibrate slightly.

'Can we break this?'

Gabe came over and looked at the table. He examined it underneath and climbed on top to look for cracks.

'Can't see how.'

Josh stepped up onto the stone beside him and looked out over the cavern.

'You're bleeding a lot,' Gabe said.

Josh looked down at his calf and saw that the cloth had become stained. A drop of blood dripped from it and hit the stone. Where it struck the granite, a tiny fissure appeared. Gabe touched it with the tip of his finger and looked up at him. Josh tore a piece from his shirt and wiped the wound. Naylor watched, his face showing interest.

Josh crouched down and wiped the bloody cloth over the fissure. He heard it crack a little. He got down and went to the wall where a rivulet of water was flowing from the ceiling. He wet the cloth and, cupping it, went back to the table. He leaned over it and wrung the sopping cloth out onto the stone. The blood ran into the crack and the table burst open, sending shards of granite across the cavern. Gabe jumped off the slab and Naylor ducked. Josh just turned his face away from the shrapnel. When he looked back the stone was broken and there was a gap large enough for him to get through.

He climbed back up and looked at the others.

'I have to go alone. Wait here and ... and pray.'

He lay down on his belly and lowered himself feet first into the crack in the stone. Gabe tried to follow him but the stone ground together above Josh's head.

Josh heard Kate cry his name but he sank downwards and didn't see her. He willed himself onwards, picturing Kate's face and nothing else. He reached his hands out to her and felt rock. He heard the sound of Kate's voice still calling his name and he tried to reach further. This time, his hands touched water and it flooded around him. He fell, turning, and went deep.

For a long moment, Josh felt suspended by the water, cocooned and motionless, his legs pulled up and his back bent. Then he kicked out and straightened his body. He forced himself through a substance that felt like syrup, thick and trying not to yield, then he burst through and swam forward. He saw eels circulating in the dim water far ahead. He didn't feel the need to breathe so he swam forward, feeling his body cutting through the water with no effort. He swam straight at the thick mass of eels and pushed through them. They parted and lashed at him. He was aware of impacts as they struck at him with their teeth and thick bodies but felt no tearing, no pain.

Kate was at their centre, caught in a twisted position, suspended and rotating slowly. He reached out to her and felt some membranous substance under his fingers. She was looking at him but wasn't moving. He used his knife to rip at whatever was holding her and felt it start to give way. He broke through the surface of it and found soft material underneath. He tore chunks of it out and the turbulence caused by the thrashing eels took it away.

Kate began to move a little and he pushed his hand through, making a hole. He just managed to touch her fingers. Immediately, she twisted her body and grabbed his hand. He pulled her and she cried out his name. It flooded out of her in a stream of bubbles and he drew her to him through the surrounding soft muck. She wrapped herself around him and he kicked for the surface. Bubbles escaped her in a steady stream as he rose. She started to panic and struggle a little and he felt his own lungs begin to scream. He closed his eyes and asked for help as he kicked hard. As his lungs let go of the last of their breath, he broke the surface.

Kate lay across his arm in the water, not breathing. He pulled her upright and thumped her back. He breathed into her mouth as best as he could while trying to keep them both afloat. She didn't respond. He hugged her hard to his chest and squeezed her, before holding her back and breathing into her mouth again. She coughed and gasped and her eyes flew open. When she saw his face, she started to cry and he held her for as long as he dared. He had to get her to shore. The eels hadn't been able to harm him when he was down there but he didn't think that the situation was going to last. He made Kate put her arms around his neck from behind and he swam towards shore, supporting her on his back.

As he swam, he tried to get his bearings. The sky had cleared. The storm was over and the moon was hanging low in the sky. He could see a glow from the town to his left.

He made it to the bank and Kate grabbed the grass. Josh pulled himself out and reached back to lift her onto the bank.

He put his arms around her.

'I knew you'd come – I knew it,' she said.

Josh kissed her wet cheek. 'Sorry it took me so long.'

'Where's Gabe?'

He pulled back from her, still holding her arms, pain radiating from his heart.

'We went under the abbey. I had to come for you by myself. The others are still down there.'

Josh looked at her and down at himself. No longer in medieval clothes, they were both wearing their normal stuff, but they were wet and dirty. He pulled up his pants leg. The echo of pain radiated from his calf, but the raw wound was gone. He straightened up, fear making him cold and stiff.

'Can you run?'

Kate nodded, her eyes wide at whatever she saw in his face. He took her hand and ran up the bank onto the road. He ran under the orange lights and cut up a lane beside the park. They ran together down the street until they reached the place where it became Abbey Street. Josh slowed down and they walked down the row of silent houses to the alley. Josh opened the gate and walked out into the open area behind the houses. He stood in the centre of the failed garden, struggling to breathe. The others were still down there, somewhere, buried in the past.

Gabe knelt on the table, his hands on the granite. Josh was gone. The stone had closed over him and sealed itself. Traces of his blood were still on the table. .

'He'll find her. They'll be okay. I know it,' he said to Naylor.

'Will he come back for us? '

Gabe didn't answer but began to walk around the chamber, looking at the walls. He found another small fissure in the wall on the opposite side to where they had entered and looked through. It was another outlet of the river. There was a lip inside the fissure but no ledge and the river was running fast below. He straightened up and walked back to Naylor at the table.

'*Where is he?*'

Gabe spun around and saw the big woman Alma step into the cavern. The young doctor was standing to one side, a knife in his hand. He was staring at the knife and

243

jerking his hand from side to side. One of the boys from the gang they had seen around town was standing beside him, watching the knife move and grinning. Alma walked into the centre of the cavern, holding herself straight and tall.

'He's close,' she said. 'Richard, come over here.'

Without taking his eyes from the weapon, Richard walked across the stone floor, stumbling a little on a jutting lip of rock. He looked up when he got to the stone table and held the knife out towards it. The knife jumped in his hand and his wrist bent as though he were divining water. He climbed onto the table and struck the knife against the traces of Josh's blood on the stone. The steel struck sparks from the rock and he looked up.

'He was here, Alma. This is his blood.'

Alma leaned over the table and touched her fingers to the stain on the stone. She brought her fingers to her face and breathed in, her eyes closed. She turned sharply to look at Gabe and he saw that her eyes were completely opaque and white. She shot her arm out, grabbed Gabe's arm and clawed at him. He hesitated for a second and then punched her in the face. She flew backwards, but stayed on her feet. Blood ran from her nose into her mouth as she laughed.

'Richard,' she said quietly.

Gabe started to turn but Richard, still on the table, reached the knife around Gabe's shoulder. Gabe got his hand up and the knife slashed across the back of it and up his arm, opening a wound like a mouth. Gabe jerked forward and pulled Richard with him. The two men fell to the floor of the cavern and Richard cried out as his elbow struck the stone. His hand remained clasped on the haft of the knife.

Gabe let him go and sprang to his feet.

The boy started to walk towards Gabe. Gabe backed away towards the fissure he had found and, as the boy lunged at him, he turned and ran for the breach in the stone. He squeezed halfway through and looked for Naylor. The man had disappeared. Gabe forced the rest of his body through, overbalanced and fell into the river.

Chapter Thirty-eight

'We're going back for them,' Kate said.

'Of course, but we need to rest while we figure out how to do it. We're both exhausted.'

Kate nodded reluctantly. 'Here?'

Josh shook his head. 'Let's get inside somewhere.'

Kate thought for a minute. 'What about Gabe's place? His mother won't mind. If she's not there, I know where he keeps his spare key and we could get some dry clothes.'

'Yeah, that's good. Just for a few minutes.'

Kate linked her arm through his and they went back out onto the street. Josh felt like he was leaving people behind again, but maybe a moment or two without having to run might let him think of something to help the others. He let Kate lead him through a couple of streets to a row of renovated houses. They were painted in clean whitewash and had timber porches.

Kate stopped at one and knocked but there was no answer. She reached up into the roof timbers of the small porch and found the key

The house smelt of Gabe. It wasn't either pleasant or unpleasant, just the individual smell a house takes from its owner.

'I'll look for some things,' Josh said. 'Do you want to hop in the shower?'

Kate agreed with evident relief and they went into the bathroom across the hall. Kate let the water run, as she had done in her own house, making sure that it didn't turn to blood. When they felt it was safe, Josh went out to look for clothes. He found Gabe's bedroom, feeling like a thief. He flipped on the light and went straight to the big wardrobe, trying not to look around. There was a picture of Kate tucked into the mirror on the door of the wardrobe. She wasn't smiling in the picture and looked like she had the weight of the world on her shoulders. She was absolutely beautiful.

He blew out a breath at the way even a picture of her could make him feel. He just needed to think. He would do whatever he had to, to make her safe, to make her happy.

He opened the door and took two T-shirts and two sweat pants out. The pants had drawstrings so they'd probably be okay. He left the room and knocked on the door of the bathroom.

'I've left some clothes out here for you. I'm going to make tea.'

'OK, I won't be long.'

Josh went downstairs, hearing the shower come on. He put on the kettle and opened doors until he found tea and biscuits and cheese. He leaned on the breakfast bar. His mind was going in circles. The abbey, the tunnel. He didn't know how he would get back to them but he wasn't leaving anyone behind.

Kate came in, dressed in Gabe's clothes. The T-shirt was huge but she had tied a knot in it and rolled up the end of the pants. Josh put his arms around her and just held her for a long moment.

'I was so afraid I'd never see you again,' he said.

'But you saved me. I knew you would.'

Josh took and released a deep breath. 'Thank God.'

He bent his head towards her as she raised her face to him. He touched his lips to hers and felt heat race through his body. Heat but more than that: emotion. For a crazy second, he felt like crying and laughing at the same time. He put his hands on her waist and pulled her close. The kiss lasted forever and was over way too fast at the same time. He looked into her eyes, amazed. She looked as surprised but she smiled quickly and pressed a quick kiss to his lips before moving out of his arms.

'You'd better go shower. Don't be long.'

He went slowly back upstairs and put his clothes into the laundry basket on top of Kate's. He stood under the hot shower and closed his eyes. The powerful stream beat at his skin and washed away the smell of the river. He kept feeling Kate's lips against his. He washed himself slowly, keeping his eyes closed. The water flowed over him and he stood there with his head down, his mind racing.

He opened his eyes and looked down at the water swirling around his feet. It went around the shower tray and disappeared down the drain. Into the sewers, through whatever system they had in the town and probably into the river eventually. Josh raised his head. He needed something that had existed in the abbot's time and that was still here now. The river was the only thing. Everything led back to the river.

He shut off the water and got out, drying himself quickly and dressing in Gabe's clothes and his own wet sneakers. The pants were slightly too short but the T-shirt was loose. He went downstairs. All the lights were off, except one small lamp in the corner of the sitting room. Kate was beside the mantelpiece, holding another picture of herself.

Josh sat down on the soft leather couch and took the picture when Kate handed it to him. She was smiling in this one. It was winter and her hair had escaped from under a white woollen hat. She was no more than twelve in the photograph and her eyes were missing the knowledge of the world that they had now. Kate sat on the arm of the couch and rested her elbow on his shoulder.

'I love Gabe, you know,' Kate said.

'I know.'

'But it's different to the way I feel about you.'

'OK.'

'I ... like you, a good bit. A lot, really.'

'I like you a lot, too.'

They smiled at each other. He pulled her down beside him on the couch. She put her arms around him and he buried his face in her hair. He was amazed, grateful, thrilled. He never wanted to let her go. He drew away, but still kept his arms around her.

'I like you more than a lot, you know,' he said.

'I know. I do too, but I have to take it slowly. Is that OK?'

'It is. But, you know, if I'm going to die or anything, you have to tell me so that I'll know.'

'OK. The same goes for me then.'

'It's a deal,' Josh said. He gave her a kiss, mostly just because he could. But he still needed to talk to her. He held her close.

'Kate, I think the only way back to them is to go in the river. I don't want to put you in any more danger. Will you please stay here? Please?'

'Have you looked outside?'

Josh frowned. 'What?'

'It's not safe here either. You have to look out the window, but don't do it here. I pulled the curtains before I put the lamp on. Come upstairs.'

Josh followed Kate upstairs. She stopped at a small window on the landing and Josh looked out through the net curtain that hung over it.

There were people in the street. They weren't young people let out of a club, but a mixture of young and old, wandering silently up and down the street. In the distance, flames rose from a roof.

'There was no one when we came in,' Kate whispered. 'What are they doing?'

'They've been sent to stop us going where we need to go, I guess.'

'We're not splitting up again.'

Josh looked at her. 'Never again,' he said.

'OK.' She smiled. 'So how are we going to get to the river?'

'Let's look and see what's at the back of these houses.'

They went back downstairs and found the back door. Josh opened it carefully on a small yard with a plastic picnic table and two chairs. The yard was surrounded by a high wall, covered in ivy. Josh brought one of the chairs over to it and stood up. There was a strip of waste ground behind the houses. Two piebald horses were asleep standing up in the rough grass. Josh hoisted himself up onto the top of the wall and put his hand down for Kate. She stood on the chair and he pulled her up beside him. He swung his legs over and dropped down the far side, almost turning his ankle on the uneven ground below. The horses moved away and Josh held his arms out for Kate. She let herself go and he caught her. She grabbed his hand and smiled at him. He grinned at her, shaking his head.

They went around the side of the little field and Josh held up barbed wire for Kate to get out under. When they were out, Josh stood for a minute then headed downhill. They made their way along the back of a retail park and cut across some narrow streets until they found a set of old steps that brought them from the top of the town to the lower level. The steps were slippery and broken. They held on to each other on the way down. At the bottom, Josh took a quick look around the corner. They were at the north end of town, above the bridge. They only had one short downhill stretch in front of them to get to the end of the old bridge.

Gabe was swept away by the pull of the river. The ceiling of the cave got lower until he was barely able to clear it. He twisted around to look ahead and saw that the ceiling met the water. He dived under and scraped his back against the roof as he was swept through a gap into a narrow tunnel. He found it hard to get a breath because the water kept crashing him under and waves broke in his face when he surfaced. The tunnel suddenly widened and he shot through into calmer water. He swam to the wall and clung to an outcrop of rock.

He looked back at the opening but no one else came through. Gabe thought that the tunnel would go right under the river to the other side. It was worth a try anyway. He let go and swam slowly to the middle of the pool, then onward towards the next passageway.

Josh and Kate ran across the street and went carefully down the little hill, keeping close to the buildings. Josh stopped at the end of the street. Something was moving on the old bridge. He put his arm across Kate to keep her against the wall and behind him. Something was uncoiling itself. It raised its head and Josh saw a thick mane running down its neck. The street lights showed a twisted human face. It dragged itself over a half-barrel full of plants and the timber collapsed under its weight. It paused and raised its head again, sniffing the air. It tilted its head towards where they stood in the small shadow of a shop awning and came towards them, dragging clay and flowers under its body.

'Kate, get to the bridge, get across the river. *Run!*'

Josh ran into the street and the great eel snapped at him, its enormous teeth cutting through the human lips and shedding blood onto Josh's back as he skidded under it. The acidic blood ate through his T-shirt and burned his skin as he ran down the beast's flank. It coiled around him and he leapt over its lashing tail to chase down the quay after Kate. Kate turned back to help him, but he waved at her that he was coming. As she ran on, the beast struck him with its head, knocking him off his feet and sending him crashing against the railing beside the river.

Gabe saw light. He had pain in a band across his chest from swimming so far. The main flow of the river branched off and he kept to a narrow by-water, moving towards the light. Then he realised with relief that he could put his feet down. The bottom was muddy and his feet sank into it. He swam a last couple of strokes and then stood again. The slope he was on was muddy but there was stone underneath. In another few steps he had the sky above his head. He climbed up onto a grassy bank and lay down.

After a while Gabe sat up and looked out over the water. He was across the river from Bailey. A timber bridge rose up not far from where he was sitting and spanned the river. Gabe stood up.

Three brigands were standing on the bank. They all had heavy knives.

Josh opened his eyes to pain. He saw the huge ugly head come speeding towards him, teeth bared. He tried to get to his feet and managed to jump sideways, but it pulled its head back and lashed at him again. It caught the loose T-shirt and pulled him off his feet. He swung for a second from its jaws before the material tore and dropped him back to the ground. He felt the wind of the beast's breath on him as it swept back in to get him.

'Noooooooooooo!'

The scream came from behind him.

He scrambled away from the beast and stood up with his back to the rail. Alma ran screaming across the road and leapt onto the eel's thick neck. Her weight knocked its head to the ground and she tore at its face. It coiled itself and pulled its head up, trying to twist backwards to bite her. She was screaming something as she tore at it. Josh shouted at her to run. Her eyes rolled white and she kept riding the beast's thrashing neck.

'*Josh!*' Kate's voice reached him and Josh turned.

She was standing at the end of the bridge. People were streaming from the side streets towards the bridge, shouting as they came. Josh ran for Kate. He grabbed her hand without slowing down and they ran onto the bridge.

One of the men came forward towards Gabe. He had

long black hair and a thick beard. He was grinning and his teeth were broken and bad, with the gleam of gold among them.

Gabe clenched his fists.

'You're not from here. This is our land,' the bearded man said.

The others separated and went on either side of Gabe.

The two men at the side came in and Gabe punched one on the jaw, knocking him sideways. The man behind him grabbed his arms and Gabe leaned forward, trying to throw him. Gabe was strong but these were adult men and tough ones at that. Gabe grabbed at him, but the first man straightened up and hit him in the temple with the butt of the big knife. Gabe staggered back onto the slope of the bank and nearly fell. The one behind him got both his arms again and hoisted them up and his friend came in and held the blade against Gabe's neck.

The bearded man walked forward and smiled at him. Gabe held his head to one side away from the blade.

'Now, do you have anything that rightly belongs to us?'

He ran rough hands over Gabe and found nothing.

'Worthless. Kill him.'

'Wait,' Gabe said.

'For what?'

'You own this side of the river.'

'I do. What of it?'

'The abbot owns the other side.'

The man spit to one side. 'He thinks he does. What do you know of it? You a friend of his?'

The knife pressed harder against Gabe's throat and he felt a trickle of blood run down his neck.

'We've been trying to get away from him and his people. We're –'

'Quiet!' The bearded man looked over at the bridge.

Gabe heard the sound of people shouting carrying across the water. The man holding him dragged him to the end of the bridge. People were crowding onto its far end.

Gabe's captors walked onto the bridge, pulling him with them.

Josh, Kate clinging to his arm, stopped when he reached the centre of the bridge, its highest point, and looked back. The crowds weren't following. They had all stopped at the end of the bridge and fallen silent. Josh could still hear Alma screaming as she struggled with the great eel.

'*Josh!*'

He spun around and saw Gabe. A man was holding him, his forearm locked under his jaw. The little group reached the centre of the bridge and stopped a few metres away. Josh kept his face impassive. Gabe was being held at knifepoint.

'What's all this?' the man holding Gabe said, raising his chin towards the now-silent crowd at the end of the bridge.

'They belong to the abbot,' Gabe said. 'He's possessed them.'

The man jerked him closer but looked at Josh. Then he frowned.

'Halley?' He shook his head.

Josh nodded.

'You're not Halley, but there's something about you that calls him to mind.

'The abbot made the dwarf kill Halley,' Josh said.

'The dwarf.'

Josh nodded.

'Halley wanted peace,' the man said. 'I just wanted the abbot gone. They amounted to the same thing.'

'I'm trying to stop the abbot. That's my friend you've got there.'

The bearded man held Josh's gaze for a moment before lowering his knife and shoving Gabe away from him.

'If ye can do it, good luck to ye.'

Josh nodded his thanks. The men turned to go.

'Ye have company,' the bearded man said, before walking away.

Josh turned and saw Naylor walking across the bridge.

Richard walked slowly down the quay in the direction Alma had taken after they left the abbey. There were people in the streets, some tearing at each other, mostly silently.

The knife was hot in Richard's hand. He was following it more than Alma. The boy had disappeared with a gang of bloodied boys who had been waiting for him outside the abbey.

Richard looked down at the knife. It was burning his

hand but it felt distant. He walked the length of the quay, looking at it. He reached the end of the bridge and saw crowds of people standing there. He passed behind them and saw Alma fighting a monstrous eel. He stopped and looked at them, frowning. He didn't understand any of this. He just knew he had one thing to do before he could go home. He wasn't entirely sure of where home was, but there was someone waiting for him, someone who needed him. The baby. He remembered the baby and felt love filling him like a bubble in his chest, a huge feeling that made it hard to breathe, but that he tried to hold on to.

Alma screamed and made him look up. She had pulled the beast to the edge of the water. She was streaming blood from multiple wounds, but she had her fingers locked under the creature's jaw and she didn't let go even when it sank its teeth into her shoulder. She pulled it backwards and disappeared over the edge of the railing. The creature's long body unwound and, pulled by her weight, slipped over the edge with her, its tail flipping up at the last minute. Richard felt as though she had pulled some weight off him as she went. He looked at the knife in his hand. He didn't want it anymore, but if he failed someone else might be taken from him. He turned back towards the end of the bridge.

Naylor walked up to Josh, looking back over his shoulder at the mob at the end of the bridge.

'How did you get out? You weren't behind me,' Gabe said.

'I waited until it was safe and then followed you.' He looked at Josh. 'You got her back. That's good. Well done.'

Josh frowned at him and gestured towards the silent crowd of people. 'How did you get through that lot?'

'They pushed me onto the bridge. I suppose we're all supposed to be together.'

Naylor stepped closer and spoke, his voice low.

'I just want to be with you, Josh. I don't mean any harm. That's okay, isn't it?'

Naylor's face was yearning and his hand was stretched out to Josh. Josh felt sorry for him and was about to tell him to join them when he saw something change in Naylor's face. There was a flash of some familiar look in his eyes. Naylor looked at him, smiling hopefully.

Josh looked away from him but gestured for him to join them.

Naylor went in behind Josh and patted him on the shoulder. Josh felt the urge to twist away from his hand but he restrained himself.

He turned to the others.

'Gabe, you and Kate go back.'

Naylor's face fell and his mouth twisted. A tear rolled down his cheek and then his brows came together in anger.

'You're always thinking about them. What about me? I didn't have to be involved in any of this. I just wanted to be your friend. And I could have been a good friend to you.'

He put his hand out to touch Josh's cheek and Josh struck the hand away.

Naylor's face changed. He lashed his head from side to side and leapt at Josh, baring his teeth. Josh was taken by surprise and fell backwards. He heard Kate scream as he fell. Naylor grabbed his shoulders and fell with him, landing on his body. Josh tried to push him off but Naylor clung to him, crying. Then his face changed again and the abbot smiled at Josh, Naylor's skin twisting to assume the shape of the abbot's features.

'Old friend, how they all cling to you! It amuses me.'

Josh struggled, but the man's body was heavy, despite being thin. The abbot pressed a kiss to Josh's lips and laughed.

Richard walked through the people. They parted before him like water. He stepped onto the bridge, his eyes on the knife again. It was vibrating in his hand. He heard voices ahead and looked up. There were people standing in the centre of the bridge. One of them was the one he was supposed to kill. He tightened his grip on the knife and went forward with more purpose.

They were all there at the arch of the bridge, standing still as though they were waiting for him. Josh and his girl. Their muscular friend was with them and also the older man, tall and thin. Richard walked faster, stepping out into the middle of the bridge. He started to run. The older man knocked Josh to the ground. The girl looked at Richard and screamed a warning. Richard felt as if time had slowed down. He heard the sound of the river and his head pulsed with an enormous throb that almost blinded him. His hand shook and he stared at the two men on the ground through a veil of red agony. Which one? He couldn't see them. He raised the knife above his head and, as it began its downward arc, he saw Lynn's sweet face. He smelt the soft scent of the baby, his son.

He watched the knife drive through the thick air as though it was being wielded by someone else. He took a deep breath that was filled with the essence of his wife and his son and forced the knife to bend to his will.

He buried the long blade in the older man's back. He twisted, screaming, and tried to grab Richard's wrist. Richard ripped the knife out and stabbed it down into the side of the man's thin throat. Blood spurted from the wound. Richard ripped the knife to one side and tore the blade across the exposed throat. He pulled the knife out and was then picked bodily up and thrown to one side by the big kid.

Richard stood up and watched as Josh rolled out from under the body and got up, wiping his face on his sleeve. Richard raised the knife again and flung it as hard as he could over the edge of the bridge. He felt the last of the terrible weight lift off him and he turned and started to walk back to the only thing that mattered anymore. The baby was safe. That was all that mattered. The baby was safe.

Naylor lay crumpled in a small dark heap. Josh stood over the body. He turned his head and looked after the young doctor who had stabbed Naylor. He had walked

261

to the end of the bridge and was facing the crowd. They pushed in around him but he started walking again and they parted before him, crying out in fury. He passed through them unharmed though they lunged at him.

Josh looked back down at Naylor's body and then at Kate.

'He was the abbot,' he said.

'Is it over? Is he gone?' she asked.

Josh shook his head. There was something wrong. He took a step away from Naylor's body as it started to vibrate. The neck twisted and abbot looked at them and smiled. He uncoiled himself and shook off Naylor's body. He stood up, leaving the body on the ground at his feet.

'Hello again, old friend.'

Josh nodded to him. 'Nicholas.'

The abbot looked at Naylor's body with distaste. 'Not worth much, but useful for observing you. He could hardly take his eyes off you in the end.'

The abbot brought his arms up from his sides in an arc. The sound of claws tearing into wood came from either side of the bridge.

Kate stood close to Josh and Gabe stood behind Kate.

The top of the rail on both sides was suddenly full of low black beasts, simpering and capering on the narrow timber, their near-human faces full of awful glee. Kate cried aloud with horror.

The abbot smiled gently at Josh.

'I told you not to oppose me. You should have paid heed.'

He brought his arms down and the beasts leapt from the rail and crashed down on them. One landed on Josh's back and as he tried to pull it off another landed higher, its long toes wrapping around his shoulders. He was knocked to the ground and they swarmed over him, holding him down. Kate's scream rang out but Josh couldn't rise to his feet. He heard the abbot say something low and, after a moment, the creatures climbed off him and he was released. He jumped to his feet.

Gabe was buried under a black carpet of squirming beasts. They surged upwards as he tried to rise but their weight knocked him back down again.

Kate lay motionless at the abbot's feet. Her face was covered in a dark membrane that looked like the skin of the black creatures. Josh took a step towards her.

The abbot raised a hand.

'You remember what I said, old friend? You wouldn't submit to my will. Now, there are no more chances.'

'There's one more,' Josh said.

The abbot raised his eyebrows.

'Take me instead.'

The abbot smiled at him.

'It's a pity we couldn't remain friends. I miss our discussions. Your mind is so clear.' He shook his head sadly. 'And you would give yourself to me? And allow this man to take what is yours?' The abbot glanced at Gabe.

Josh nodded.

The abbot laughed. 'No, my friend, the bargain is uneven.'

He raised his hands again and the black veil over Kate's face started to spread over her body. Josh tried to get to her but it felt like there was a wall in front of him. The black cobwebbing covered her and then sank to the ground and she was gone. The abbot turned and walked away. Josh was able to move forward again and he ran for the abbot, but within a few steps he couldn't see him anymore. He turned around, his hands in his hair. They were gone.

The creatures that had held Gabe on the ground were gone as well and Gabe was getting slowly to his feet. Josh ran to him.

'What the hell happened? Where's Kate?' Gabe said.

'He took her. We have to get back to the abbey.' Josh turned and ran toward the end of the bridge to get back into town. The crowd was still there, blocking his way. The gang of boys stepped forward from the crowd and faced Josh.

Gabe put his hand on his arm. 'C'mon, we're not going that way.'

Josh let himself be pulled back. They ran back along the bridge.

At the end of the bridge, the trio of brigands were waiting for them. Their bearded leader looked at Josh, head on one side.

'He took your woman.'

Josh nodded. 'Will you get me across the river? I have to get to the abbey.'

'Both of us,' Gabe said.

The bearded man looked at them, sucking his teeth.

'Ye can have the use of a boat. Leave it well downriver so we can get it back. There's a backwater behind a great white rock. You won't miss it. Pull her in there.'

Josh agreed and he and Gabe followed the men down the riverbank. They pulled off the branches and reeds hiding a small boat and pulled it down to the water. Gabe and Josh got in and the men pushed them out. Josh took the oars and started rowing downriver.

He rowed well beyond the town and he and Gabe were silent until Gabe saw the white rock. Josh looked over his shoulder and then steered the boat to the shore. He was able to row a little longer up the backwater and then Gabe jumped out and Josh put the oars at the bottom of the boat. He jumped out and he and Gabe pulled the boat into the reeds.

They walked up the bank together and picked their way over marshy ground until they came to a track in the rushes. Josh knew they weren't in modern Bailey anymore. There was a different feel about the place. They walked in silence for a while, keeping a distance between them.

Josh glanced at Gabe.

'Thanks for coming with me.'

'I'm not doing it for you,' Gabe answered.

Josh stopped and faced him.

'Look, I get it. You're doing it for Kate, I'm doing it for Kate. I'm sorry that it came to a choice between us, but I'm never going to be sorry that she's with me. I also know that if we get through this, she's going to want you in her life. You and I are just going to have to figure this out and deal with it.'

265

'Maybe that damn monk will take you out of the picture and I won't have to worry about it,' Gabe said.

Josh nodded. 'Maybe.' He raised an eyebrow at Gabe. 'But the way this town works, I could probably still hang around, dead or not.'

Gabe's lips twitched and he shook his head. He looked towards the town and then back at Josh. 'Just what I need. Another bloody ghost.'

Josh grinned and held out his hand. Gabe pursed his lips and then shook it.

'Let's go find her,' Josh said.

Gabe nodded and they climbed the bank ahead of them. They saw the rough road and the outskirts of town in the soft pre-dawn light. Colour was creeping into the sky.

When they reached the first buildings, Josh slowed down and went carefully, keeping close to the cottages and then the merchant's houses. As they approached the abbey, Josh felt a light pierce his eyes, shooting pain deep into his head and down his neck. He staggered against a building and Gabe grabbed his arm.

'What's wrong?' Gabe said.

'It's Halley. Something's happening.'

Josh straightened up and winced. He was more aware of Halley now than ever before. It felt like there was an echo of him in his mind all the time.

'I'm OK,' he said. 'C'mon, let's go in.'

'What about those monks inside? I don't have my knife anymore.'

'I think we'll just have to go on faith. Maybe that's all

the knives were for anyway, something physical to hang onto.'

'Still, wait a second.' Gabe went back down the street and scouted about. When he came back he was carrying a stout stick and stripping leaves off it. He hefted it for weight and grinned at Josh.

'I'll put my faith in this as well, just to be safe.'

They went through the entrance door of the abbey. The morning light started to find its way into the hall. There were shadows and movements around the edges of the hall, but nobody came forward. Josh turned to the wall that had opened for him before. It was solid and he couldn't breach it without the knife.

'Let's look around the rest of the building. Maybe there's another way down,' Gabe said.

Josh nodded, conscious of the echo in his mind. He looked up at the ceiling.

'I don't think they're down there. I think they're somewhere close.'

He walked around the hall and found the way to the abbey's chapel. They went through the doors.

There were no seats, just stone benches against the walls. There were big stone pillars running down either side of the central area. There were a few golden beeswax candles burning, producing a faint scent of honey. Josh walked down the centre of the nave with Gabe behind him. He stopped at the top and looked around. There were two areas hidden from the nave by chancel screens. He turned around and looked back down the body of the chapel. Monks were filing slowly into the room, but they paid no attention to Josh and Gabe, seeming not to see them. They began to sing and Josh felt the vibration of a memory that didn't belong to him. It was the 'Dies Irae', the Day of Wrath. Judgement Day. The sound echoed through the chapel as the monks sat down on the bare floor, still singing the Gregorian chant.

Quid sum miser tunc dicturus, quem patronum rogaturus, cum vix iustus sit securus? The Latin swam around him and he understood it in his heart. *What am I the wretch then to say, what patron I to beseech, when scarcely the just be secure*?

Halley was with him and Josh felt tears rise in his eyes. He felt Halley's terrible sadness for his friend, who had turned so far from the path, who had adopted evil in his greed and quest for power. His own terror for Kate threatened to overwhelm him and the half memory of Halley's spirit being defeated over and over again made him feel helpless in the face of what was to come. He put his fists against his forehead in despair. Halley, whether Josh's ancestor or spiritual twin, was a good man but a gentle one. He had only ever wanted peace. Josh knew it was his passiveness that always saw him defeated.

Josh saw himself as a boy, accepting everything that came his way, trying to be a good boy to make everyone happy, to make his parents look at him the way they looked at Callum. But Callum and so many others were dead. But he himself was still here. Since he had met Kate, he had changed. Instead of towing the line, he had been fighting back, standing up for the people he loved.

And Kate was going to die for the abbot's pleasure if

Josh failed, if he didn't face the ordeal ahead and overcome it. He straightened up and took a deep breath. He wasn't going to fail. He couldn't.

The monks' voices faded away on the last stanzas of the holy chant. *Confutatis maledictis, flammis acribus addictis, voca me cum benedictis. After the accursed have been silenced, given up to the bitter flames, call me with the blessed.*

Josh turned around and faced the chancel screen. An image of a crucifix was on the screen separating the presbytery from the nave of the church.

Josh's view of the world had been destroyed. In a very short space of time he had lost his beloved big brother to the river, had lost his parents to their silent grief, but he had found Kate. In one week, he had discovered where he belonged and who he belonged to. He loved Kate more than anything. Evil existed here as a physical force, beyond newspaper headlines and philosophical arguments and he had to find a way to destroy it to save her.

Josh looked up at again at the crucifix. If evil existed, then good had to as well. He saw it in Kate's face and even Gabe's, whose love was written all over him. He looked at the face of Christ on the cross and silently asked for help, then looked over at Gabe, who was waiting for him. Gabe now knew he had no hope of Kate returning his love in the way he wanted but he was still here, putting himself in danger.

'The presbytery is the most holy place in the abbey,' Josh said. 'He's corrupted it. That's where they'll be.'

Josh walked over to Gabe.

'Can I borrow that for a minute?' he asked, nodding at Gabe's staff.

'Sure, what's up?'

Josh stepped back.

Please God help me not to kill him, he thought. He swung the branch as hard as he could. He struck Gabe in the side of the head and the vibration from the blow cracked the stick and sent a shot of pain up to Josh's shoulder. He dropped the staff as Gabe crashed to the ground. Josh leaned over him. He was out, but breathing evenly.

Josh walked up to the screen and slipped past it into the presbytery. The stone altar lay on the easternmost side of the church. The abbot sat in a large ornate throne. Kate was lying in front of the altar. Her face was free of the black veil and she began to struggle when she saw Josh, crying his name, but she couldn't get up.

'You're welcome, old friend.' The abbot got up and put his hand on Josh's shoulder. He walked around him and stood to face him again. 'I knew you would come of course. I haven't taken my pleasure yet.'

The abbot clapped his hands and the black creatures swarmed in from the dark edges of the room. There were thick eels among them, slithering across the stone floor.

'But now that you're here to observe ...'

The abbot clapped his hands once more and the creatures swarmed over Kate. Josh ran to her and started pulling them off, throwing them aside, frenzied. He knocked enough of them away to throw himself over her, putting his arms around her head. Kate curled up under him. With his face close to hers, he could hear her muffled cries of horror.

The creatures swarmed over Josh's back. He straightened up with difficulty against their weight. He stretched his arms out and gripped the edge of the altar, forming a protective shelter over Kate. He felt heat in his body radiate outwards into his limbs. He closed his eyes and pushed the heat, tensing his muscles. He heard a crack like lightning and opened his eyes. The creatures were thrown off him. There was light all around him. Kate had her eyes closed against its brightness. Josh stared at it then looked up.

The abbot had moved to stand in front of the altar and was staring at him with fury twisting his face.

The abbot clapped his hands again, but Josh could only hear the sound of his own steady breathing. He kept looking at the abbot but out of the corner of his eye he could see the creatures beginning to come at him again, the eels contorting themselves and twisting closer to him. He knew that he could keep Kate safe from the onslaught but that he would suffer. He looked at her one last time, took a deep breath and closed his eyes.

'Domine, miserere nobis,' he said. *Lord, have mercy on us.*

The creatures tore at him, ripping into his flesh. The agony made the shield around Kate stronger, the light brighter. He screamed and the abbot laughed.

The light was too bright to open her eyes, but Kate had an overwhelming feeling that she needed to. She squinted them open and shielded her eyes with her hand. Josh was above her, his face agonised. He screamed but the sound of it didn't reach her. Kate tried to touch him but there was something between them. She saw a black creature rise up on his shoulder and swoop its head down on him, burying its teeth in the back of his neck. She screamed then. She couldn't take her eyes off his beautiful face, tormented. He held fast above her and Kate understood that, somehow, he was shielding her. She could see now that the creatures were swamping him. Despite the agony, he opened his eyes and looked down at her. She remembered their deal and knew it was time.

'I love you, Josh.'

His lips formed the words and he held her gaze for one last moment before his eyes closed and his chin fell to his chest. The shield held fast and Josh's body leaned on it, lifeless. Kate saw the abbot circling, his face contorted. He kicked away the creatures covering Josh's body and they all swept away into the shadows. The abbot grabbed Josh's body and threw it onto the stone floor. He ran to it and started to pull and tear at it. The black creatures scampered around him, giggling and snapping at the body.

Kate was free of the shield and stood up. She wanted desperately to go to Josh, wanted to save his body from further torment, even if he couldn't feel it anymore, but he had sacrificed himself for her and she couldn't let it be in vain. She ran to the chancel screen and slammed into Gabe. There was a trickle of blood running from his temple. He held her against his chest and they looked back into the presbytery.

All at once, light began to emanate from Josh's body. The abbot didn't notice at first but his creatures pulled back, baring their teeth and squealing. Then the light blossomed and flared and the abbot fell back, staring at it. It rose into the room and began to swirl around the abbot. Kate could see him striking out, trying to get free of it, but he was trapped inside it. He fell on the ground and held out his hand in defence. The light stilled and hovered over him. Kate could see a face in it, a shape. It was Josh and yet not him. The blue eyes were the same.

'Halley,' Gabe whispered.

Kate saw a smile form on the face. Then the light seemed to concentrate and arrow and it plunged into the abbot. He held still for one second until the light burst from him and he fragmented, bloodlessly. One moment he was there, the next the room exploded with light and Kate had to turn her face away. When it faded, they were blind for a few minutes and held onto each other.

When Kate's vision came back, she turned to look at the room. The abbot and his creatures were gone and Josh's body lay alone on the floor. She rushed to him, Gabe following.

She turned him onto his back and put her left arm around him and tried to lift him. She couldn't bear to leave him lying on the cold floor. His face was mostly undamaged but the rest of his poor body was torn and broken. Gabe went behind and helped her to hold him up. Kate barely noticed. Her heart was pierced and her sorrow too bitter to bear. She put her cheek to his beloved face and cried.

He was on the bow of Halley's ship. The Zephyros *was at sea again and the crew were running over her decks, working her and joking with each other. Josh turned and looked at Halley. The captain smiled at him.*

'We're under sail, Josh. There is no greater feeling in the world.'

Josh smiled back and looked down over the sturdy lines of the little ship. She was flying over the white-topped water. Seagulls wheeled above her mast. Josh felt completely at home on her deck. He looked at Halley.

'Will you ever come back, do you think?' he said.

'Back to Bailey?' Halley turned his face to the wind and took a deep breath, his eyes closed. He shook his head and looked back at Josh. 'I'll follow the good winds, wherever they go. There's no need to go back to Bailey ever again.'

He looked down along his ship. A girl came up from below and smiled at him, her hair flowing in the breeze. She bore a startling resemblance to Kate.

Halley raised his hand to wave to her and turned his peaceful smile on Josh.

'No need to ever go back,' Halley said. 'And how about you?'

'It's my home. And Kate is there.'

Halley clapped him on the shoulder and nodded.

'I know what that feels like. This ship was ever my home.'

He was silent for a moment. Josh saw his brows draw together.

'Just remember, Josh, the skin between Bailey and what lies

beyond this world is thin.'

Josh frowned. Halley put his hand on his shoulder and went on.

'If you ever need me, you can call me,' he said. He looked at the girl standing amidships and then back at Josh. 'But only if you really need to.' He grinned at Josh and the dream began to fade. The Zephyros *took the wind in her sails and disappeared.*

Kate gradually became aware of light. She didn't want to open her eyes. She could feel Josh's still body in her arms and she didn't want to look at his beautiful face and see no life there. She tried to make herself go back into the daze or sleep she had been in but couldn't. She squeezed her eyes tighter and tried to force the memory away. She was just lying on her bed and Josh was asleep in her arms. If she never opened her eyes again, she could keep pretending.

But she wasn't good at pretending. She bit her lip and forced her eyes open. There was rough damp grass under her instead of stone. They were back in the abandoned garden and the pink and gold of dawn filled the sky.

She moved back slightly, supporting Josh's head. She let Gabe lower him to the grass and then leaned over the body and kissed Josh's lips. They were still warm. The light of dawn made him look as though there was a glow of life in his cheeks but he was completely still.

Kate put her head on Josh's chest and cried silently. Gabe came around and knelt on the ground beside her. He put his big warm hand on her back.

Kate touched Josh's cheek. The sun was shining on his

275

face and hair and he felt and looked so warm and present. She couldn't believe that he was gone. She shook her head. She was numb.

Gabe took her hand. They entwined their fingers over his body, resting their hands on his chest. They sat that way for a long time.

Kate thought that Gabe had moved and glanced up at him. He had his eyes closed. This time when Kate felt the movement, Gabe looked up. They looked at each other and they both felt it when his chest rose slightly.

Kate looked at Josh's face. He let out a long sigh as if he had been holding his breath for a long time. Kate gasped and let Gabe go. She took Josh's hand and held it with both of hers. He lay still for a long time, just breathing. The sun was fully risen when he opened his eyes. He winced against the light and Kate moved to block the sun for him.

Josh brought Kate's hands to his chest and held them there.

'Halley's gone,' he said, tapping his chest with their joined hands.

She nodded, catching her breath and trying not cry. 'The abbot too. And you're back. It's finally over now, isn't it?'

'Yeah. It's over.'

With their help, Josh sat up. He was in a lot of pain, but the grievous wounds had diminished. Some of the worst ones were healing even as Kate looked at them.

They helped him out through the alley, over the street and down Sugar Lane. Then Kate made him sit on a bench on the quay front while Gabe went to fetch the car from the cottage, which he promised to drive slowly.

Kate sat beside Josh and put her arms gently around him.

'You saved us,' she said. 'You defeated him.'

Josh shook his head. 'I needed Halley to help me save you and he needed me to finally defeat the abbot. He had his destiny. I had mine.'

Kate rested her head lightly on his shoulder.

'What day is it?' he said.

'Saturday.'

He paused for a long moment.

'It's been an interesting week.'

Kate looked up and smiled at him. 'Just you wait for next week.'

By the time they got him to the cottage Josh was almost asleep. Gabe helped him up the stairs and he fell into Kate's bed.

Josh was conscious that there was someone in the room for a while, some tugging at his clothes and then a light covering came down over his body and he was gone.

Josh slept for hours and woke up ravenous. He was alone in Kate's room. A smell of bacon frying wafted under his nose and his stomach growled. He sat up and groaned. Every inch of him ached. He looked himself over. He seemed to be put together okay, but he had faint scars in a lot of places. He stood up and his knees popped. He made his way to the bathroom and stood under the shower for a long time. When he got out, he felt better. Someone had brought some of his clothes from home and had left jeans, a T-shirt, boxers and runners on a chair. He got dressed and went downstairs. There was breakfast debris all over the kitchen table and Kate was standing with her back to him, making sausages squeak on the pan. His stomach growled again, very loudly, making him wince. Kate was wearing a white sleeveless blouse that ended above the top of her jeans. Her skin was creamy and beautiful. She turned, saw him and dropped the spatula. They met in the middle of the kitchen.

He wrapped his arms around her and breathed her in. She stayed pressed against him for a long time until he finally drew away. He put his hands on her face and kissed her. It was the beginning of everything.

Chapter Thirty-nine

Richard took a bus back to the hospital and when he went in the nurses made a fuss of him. He must have looked bad because they fetched him food and made him lie down in a spare bed in the day ward. When he woke up, he felt a wave of grief wash over him for Lynn. But it made him feel clean. It felt right to grieve for her. He got to his feet and went to get his son.

Gabe left after breakfast and went to find out what had happened. It seemed the whole town had gone crazy. There had been multiple fires and accidents. He went home and found a note from his mother saying she'd be back after the weekend.

He stood for a time in the bedroom where the fetch had come to him. It hadn't been Kate and the experience had been all wrong, but it was the only memory he had of holding her, of being with her. It wasn't a good memory to hold on to, but he let himself experience it just once.

He took Kate's picture from the corner of the mirror and looked at it. He should probably put it away. It no longer represented hope. But, instead, he put it back in its usual place. He still loved her and he reckoned love wasn't such a bad thing, even if she didn't love him the same as he loved her. Besides, maybe it was just a matter of time. He had always been there for her and if she broke up with Josh he would still be there. Maybe all he had to do was wait. He could do that.

Everything was all fresh and new. The storm had taken the heat with it but it was still a pleasant day. Kate walked up to the edge of the river. A little fish jumped after a fly and made a ripple as he fell back into the water. There were already a couple of pleasure boats out. She sat up on the lock gate and swung her feet out over the water. Josh sat beside her. She wanted to tell him lots and kiss him lots. Another little fish jumped for his breakfast.

Adam went home and ignored his mother when she called to him from the kitchen to ask where he had been. He went to the bathroom and locked the door. He put his hands on the edge of the sink and looked at himself in the mirror on the medicine cabinet. He had stubble on his chin and black rings under his eyes. He picked at his jaw. He had dried flecks of blood on him. He had a half memory of a wild trip, lasting a long time. He thought he might have done some terrible things. He frowned at himself in the mirror, trying to remember what had happened. He needed to figure out if he was in trouble. The blood wasn't his and he felt like he had been in a fight. His jaw ached.

An image of woman flashed through his mind. Her lips were bleeding. He shook his head. The picture was horrible but it got a little surge of pleasure from it. He looked at himself again. The idea that it was bad to get excited at pain and blood occurred to him. He knew it wasn't normal to feel like that. He opened the cabinet's double doors and saw his face split as the doors separated. He rooted around for something he could take for the ache in his jaw, but his gaze fell on a packet of razors. He stared at them, transfixed.

His mother knocked on the door of the bathroom. She asked him if he was alright. He didn't answer. He just kept looking at the razors.

He picked the packet up and took a razor out. He threw the packet back into the cabinet and shut the doors. He put the blade in the centre of his palm. It lay there, looking alive. He picked it up carefully in his fingers and brought the edge to his wrist. He pressed the corner of the metal to his skin and pushed until a drop of blood appeared. He looked at it. It grew a bit fatter and then stopped and just sat on his skin. He rubbed the side of his hand over it and smeared it across the blue veins of his wrist.

The blade would slip through his skin as if it was warm butter. He looked at the smear and brought the blade back to his wrist. He touched it to the biggest blue vein. He looked at himself in the mirror for a long time and then grinned.

'Fuck that,' he said.

He threw the blade into the sink and went to his room for a sleep. It was Saturday and he had that blonde to chase tonight.

Chapter Forty

Naylor's apartment stood silent and empty until the rent came due. His landlord finally came to investigate why it hadn't been paid. He knocked and there was no answer. When there was no answer for three days in a row, he let himself in. There had been no smell in the hall, but he was still convinced that he would find Doc Naylor on the floor. He had vaguely heroic visions of himself ringing the police and telling the story. The only trouble was the visions ended with him hiring specialist cleaning firms for the stains on the timber. That wasn't such a good story. So he opened the door carefully, not knowing what he wanted to find.

Everything was in order. All Naylor's stuff was still lying around but in his experience as a landlord, he reckoned that if the clothes were gone, then Naylor had done a bunk. He went into the bedroom to check. He didn't get as far as the wardrobe.

The bed and the walls were mostly bare except for three drawings. The face was the same in all three, though from different angles and in various lights. The landlord knew nothing about art, but these all looked to be pretty good. They weren't like that modern stuff anyway.

But the subject of them. He had always wondered about Naylor and these pictures confirmed his suspicions. They were all of a handsome young man. Most of them were just of his face but some showed his bare shoulders. The landlord put his face close to one of the pencil drawings.

The overall picture was very simple. It was just the young man's face turned slightly so that most of his face was shown catching the light. The landlord held it closer to his face and shifted his glasses higher on his nose. He frowned at it and squinted his eyes. It was made up of thousands of tiny lines, each thin pencil mark intersecting the next one perfectly. If Naylor had done these, he had taken a lot of care. This one looked like the work of many hours. The landlord didn't know much about this kind of work, but he knew obsession when he saw it. And also maybe love. When he was telling the story in the pub he would leave out the part about love, but as he looked over the drawings, it was obvious in each one. Love, plain and simple.

The fisherman went out early and bailed the storm water out of his boat. He checked that she was sound and stowed his bag under the cubby at the bow and his rod on the bottom of the boat. He was heading out for a full day of Sunday fishing. Nothing better. He had his wife's best chicken salad sandwiches and a few cans of beer. He was going to his favourite spot where it was nice and shady, but there was always a breeze so the few flies wouldn't bother him. He would hang the beers on a rope over the side to make them cool. He didn't even care if he didn't catch anything, although it was nice to bring a few fresh fish home to the missus for dinner.

He cast off and started his little outboard engine. He often thought of getting a loan for a bigger boat, one with a cabin, maybe one with an inboard engine. The wife was always saying she would come with him for a day out if he had a bigger boat. He couldn't tell her, but he liked being out by himself. And he liked being so close to the water. It wouldn't be the same in a bigger boat.

Today was a special day too. He hadn't been out for ages. The river had felt sort of wrong for the last little while. Sort of spooky. But today was a glorious day. A perfect day for getting back on the water. His little old Seagull engine was puttering along fine. She was ancient but he kept her in good working order and started her regularly over the winter in a barrel in the back yard.

He was almost at his fishing spot when he saw something on the mud. He squinted at it and couldn't figure it out. Something had got caught up in the storm and was now fetched up on the mud in the low tide. He went on past it and got to his sweet spot. He put out his little anchor and tied the beer cans on the rope and chucked them into the water.

He got himself all set up and sat back to wait for a bite. The dead heat was gone out of the day since the storm but it was still going to be lovely.

He got to thinking of the thing he had seen on the mud. He couldn't imagine what it was. It was unlike anything he had ever seen on the river before and it worried him a bit. He tried to put it out of his mind but as the day wore on and he didn't catch anything worthwhile, he thought maybe he'd take a spin back that way a bit earlier than he had planned.

Once he had the thought, it was difficult to shift it. He fished for another little while and only caught a little trout that he threw back. He couldn't settle so he pulled up the beers and the anchor and started the engine.

It took longer going back because the tide was coming in. He began to think that the thing would be totally immersed in water before he got there but as he rounded a curve in the river, he saw it lying in the mud, water only half covering it.

He stopped the engine when he got close enough and dropped his anchor again. He got his boathook from the bottom of the boat and leaned out. He prodded the thing a little. It was solid but sort of soft. He poked it again and shrieked when it moved. He slid to the other side of the boat and nearly tipped her. The thing on the mud rolled over and he saw what it was.

She lay there for a minute and then started to struggle to sit up. She was mostly covered with mud but she had blood on her as well. He rooted in his bag for his mobile phone and pulled it out to call an ambulance. He hoped they would be able to find the place and that they would come soon. He didn't think he'd be able to manage such a big girl all by himself.

Chapter Forty-one

Josh walked into the graveyard. Kate squeezed his hand. The gravestone wasn't up yet. He knew that they had to wait until the ground had settled. There was a wooden cross with a temporary plaque on it instead. He used the end of his T-shirt to wipe raindrops off the plaque.

Callum Ryan 1998 – 2018.

'He was ...' He stopped.

Kate tucked her arm into his.

He couldn't say anymore. Callum had been a good brother, a good person. Maybe in time he'd be able to say those things out loud, but for now they were too big and caught in his throat. He squeezed her arm and after a moment they turned around and headed for the gate. The graveyard was on the hill above town, edged by the start of the woods.

A movement caught Josh's eyes and he stopped. A

deer stepped out of the wood and gazed at him. He was certain it was the same deer that had led him through the woods when he was being chased by the dead of the river. She looked sharp and alert and the skin on her flank was trembling. Her eyes were wide, showing white.

All at once, Josh was following her into the wood. She ran deeper and deeper until she stopped at a cool grove in the middle of large trees. A huge oak dominated the space, larger than all the others. There was blood on the trunk of the tree, pouring from a hole in the thick bark. The deer turned her head to look at him before fleeing deeper into the wood, making a strange cry as she did so. A magpie answered with its coarse voice.

The image wavered, leaving only the dark red of the blood.

It's not over.

Josh blinked and realised that Kate was shaking his arm. He was still standing in the graveyard.

'Josh, what is it?'

He couldn't speak, but he saw by her face that she knew.

It's not over.

Epilogue

Bailey's historic old streets wind and climb and it has alleys and long sets of steps leading from the lower town to the upper. It sits on the edge of the river, backed by a steep hill, crowded with deep woodland.

It has charm and a combination of ancient and modern that make it a pleasant and interesting place to live. And like any town, it has both bright and dark about it.

If you enjoyed this book from
Poolbeg why not visit our website

www.poolbeg.com

and get another book delivered straight
to your home or to a friend's home.

All books despatched within 24 hours.

Free postage on orders over €25*

Why not join our mailing list at
www.poolbeg.com and get some
fantastic offers, competitions,
book giveaways, author interviews, new releases
and much more?

 @PoolbegBooks

 www.facebook.com/poolbegpress

 poolbegbooks

*Free postage over €25 applies to Ireland only